MARY SHELLEY

Transformation
and Other Stories

Legend Press Ltd, 51 Gower Street, London, WC1E 6HJ
info@legendpress.co.uk | www.legendpress.co.uk

Print ISBN 978-1-91716-3-927
Ebook ISBN 978-1-91716-3-934
Set in Times.

Mary Shelley was born in 1797, the only daughter of William Godwin the philosopher and writer and Mary Wollstonecraft, the radical author of *A Vindication of the Rights of Woman*. Her mother died a few days after her birth.

In 1814 she left England with Percy Bysshe Shelley, and married him in 1816 on the death of his wife. She returned to England in 1823 after her husband's death. Shelley is best remembered as the author of *Frankenstein*, but she wrote several other works including novels, biographies and short stories. She died in 1851.

CONTENTS

Transformation

"Forthwith this frame of mine was wrench'd
With a woful agony,
Which forced me to begin my tale,
And then it set me free.

"Since then, at an uncertain hour,
That agony returns;
And till my ghastly tale is told
This heart within me burns."

– Coleridge's Ancient Mariner.

I have heard it said, that, when any strange, supernatural, and necromantic adventure has occurred to a human being, that being, however desirous he may be to conceal the same, feels at certain periods torn up as it were by an intellectual earthquake, and is forced to bare the inner depths of his spirit to another. I am a witness of the truth of this. I have dearly sworn to myself never to reveal to human ears the horrors to which I once, in excess of fiendly pride, delivered myself over. The holy man who heard my confession, and reconciled me to the Church, is dead. None knows that once—
Why should it not be thus? Why tell a tale of impious tempting of Providence, and soul-subduing humiliation? Why? answer

7

me, ye who are wise in the secrets of human nature! I only know that so it is; and in spite of strong resolve, – of a pride that too much masters me – of shame, and even of fear, so to render myself odious to my species, – I must speak.

Genoa! my birthplace – proud city! looking upon the blue Mediterranean – dost thou remember me in my boyhood, when thy cliffs and promontories, thy bright sky and gay vineyards, were my world? Happy time! when to the young heart the narrow-bounded universe, which leaves, by its very limitation, free scope to the imagination, enchains our physical energies, and, sole period in our lives, innocence and enjoyment are united. Yet, who can look back to childhood, and not remember its sorrows and its harrowing fears? I was born with the most imperious, haughty, tameless spirit. I quailed before my father only; and he, generous and noble, but capricious and tyrannical, at once fostered and checked the wild impetuosity of my character, making obedience necessary, but inspiring no respect for the motives which guided his commands. To be a man, free, independent; or, in better words, insolent and domineering, was the hope and prayer of my rebel heart.

My father had one friend, a wealthy Genoese noble, who in a political tumult was suddenly sentenced to banishment, and his property confiscated. The Marchese Torella went into exile alone. Like my father, he was a widower: he had one child, the almost infant Juliet, who was left under my father's guardianship. I should certainly have been unkind to the lovely girl, but that I was forced by my position to become her protector. A variety of childish incidents all tended to one point, – to make Juliet see in me a rock of defence; I in her, one who must perish through the soft sensibility of her nature too rudely visited, but for my guardian care. We grew up together. The opening rose in May was not more sweet than this dear girl. An irradiation of beauty was spread over her face. Her form, her step, her voice – my heart weeps even now, to think of all of relying, gentle, loving, and pure, that she enshrined. When I was eleven and Juliet eight years of age, a cousin of mine, much older than either – he seemed to us a man – took great notice of my playmate; he called her his bride, and asked her to marry him. She refused, and he insisted, drawing her unwillingly towards him. With the countenance and emotions of a maniac I threw myself on him – I strove to draw his sword – I clung to his neck with the ferocious resolve to strangle him: he was obliged to call for assistance to disengage himself from me. On that night I led Juliet to the chapel of our house: I made her touch the sacred relics – I harrowed her child's heart, and profaned her child's lips with an oath, that she would be mine, and mine only.

Well, those days passed away. Torella returned in a few years, and became wealthier and more prosperous than ever. When I was seventeen, my father died; he had been magnificent to prodigality; Torella rejoiced that my minority would afford an opportunity for repairing my fortunes. Juliet and I had been affianced beside my father's deathbed – Torella was to be a second parent to me.

I desired to see the world, and I was indulged. I went to Florence, to Rome, to Naples; thence I passed to Toulon, and at length reached what had long been the bourne of my wishes, Paris. There was wild work in Paris then. The poor king, Charles the Sixth, now sane, now mad, now a monarch, now an abject slave, was the very mockery of humanity. The queen, the dauphin, the Duke of Burgundy, alternately friends and foes, – now meeting in prodigal feasts, now shedding blood in rivalry, – were blind to the miserable state of their country, and the dangers that impended over it, and gave themselves wholly up to dissolute enjoyment or savage strife. My character still followed me. I was arrogant and self-willed; I loved display, and above all, I threw off all control. My young friends were eager to foster passions which furnished them with pleasures. I was deemed handsome – I was master of every knightly accomplishment. I was disconnected with any political party. I grew a favourite with all: my presumption and arrogance was pardoned in one so young: I became a spoiled child. Who could control me? not the letters and advice of Torella – only strong necessity visiting me in the abhorred shape of an empty purse. But there were means to refill this void. Acre after acre, estate after estate, I sold. My dress, my jewels, my horses and their caparisons, were almost unrivalled in gorgeous Paris, while the lands of my inheritance passed into possession of others.

The Duke of Orleans was waylaid and murdered by the Duke of Burgundy. Fear and terror possessed all Paris. The dauphin and the queen shut themselves up; every pleasure was suspended. I grew weary of this state of things, and my heart yearned for my boyhood's haunts. I was nearly a beggar, yet still I would go there, claim my bride, and rebuild my fortunes. A few happy ventures as a merchant would make me rich again. Nevertheless, I would not return in humble guise. My last act was to dispose of my remaining estate near Albaro for half its worth, for ready money. Then I despatched all kinds of artificers, arras, furniture of regal splendour, to fit up the last relic of my inheritance, my palace in Genoa. I lingered a little longer yet, ashamed at the part of the prodigal returned, which I feared I should play. I sent my horses. One matchless Spanish jennet I despatched to my promised bride: its caparisons flamed with jewels and cloth of gold. In every part I caused to be entwined the initials of Juliet and her Guido. My present found favour in hers and in her father's eyes.

Still to return a proclaimed spendthrift, the mark of impertinent wonder, perhaps of scorn, and to encounter singly the reproaches or taunts of my fellow-citizens, was no alluring prospect. As a shield between me and censure, I invited some few of the most reckless of my comrades to accompany me: thus I went armed against the world, hiding a rankling feeling, half fear and half penitence, by bravado.

I arrived in Genoa. I trod the pavement of my ancestral palace. My proud step was no interpreter of my heart, for I deeply felt that, though surrounded by every luxury, I was a beggar. The first step I took in claiming Juliet must widely declare me such. I read contempt or pity in the looks of all. I fancied that rich and poor, young and old, all regarded me with derision. Torella came not near me. No wonder that my second father should expect a son's deference from me in waiting first on him. But, galled and stung by a sense of my follies and demerit, I strove to throw the blame on others. We kept nightly orgies in Palazzo Carega. To sleepless, riotous nights followed listless, supine mornings. At the Ave Maria we showed our dainty persons in the streets, scoffing at the sober citizens, casting insolent glances on the shrinking women. Juliet was not among them – no, no; if she had been there, shame would have driven me away, if love had not brought me to her feet.

I grew tired of this. Suddenly I paid the Marchese a visit. He was at his villa, one among the many which deck the suburb of San Pietro d'Arena. It was the month of May, the blossoms of the fruit-trees were fading among thick, green foliage; the vines were shooting forth; the ground strewed with the fallen olive blooms; the firefly was in the myrtle hedge; heaven and earth wore a mantle of surpassing beauty. Torella welcomed me kindly, though seriously; and even his shade of displeasure soon wore away. Some resemblance to my father – some look and tone of youthful ingenuousness, softened the good old man's heart. He sent for his daughter – he presented me to her as her betrothed. The chamber became hallowed by a holy light as she entered. Hers was that cherub look, those large, soft eyes, full dimpled cheeks, and mouth of infantine sweetness, that expresses the rare union of happiness and love. Admiration first possessed me; she is mine! was the second proud emotion, and my lips curled with haughty triumph. I had not been the *enfant gâté* of the beauties of France not to have learnt the art of pleasing the soft heart of woman. If towards men I was overbearing, the deference I paid to them was the more in contrast. I commenced my courtship by the display of a thousand gallantries to Juliet, who, vowed to me from infancy, had never admitted the devotion of others; and who, though accustomed to expressions of admiration, was uninitiated in the language of lovers.

For a few days all went well. Torella never alluded to my extravagance; he treated me as a favourite son. But the time came, as we discussed the preliminaries to my union with his daughter, when this fair face of things should be overcast. A contract had been drawn up in my father's lifetime. I had rendered this, in fact, void by having squandered the whole of the wealth which was to have been shared by Juliet and myself. Torella, in consequence, chose to consider this bond as cancelled, and proposed another, in which, though the wealth he bestowed was immeasurably increased, there were so many restrictions as to the mode of spending it, that I, who saw independence only in free career being given to my own imperious will, taunted him as taking advantage of my situation, and refused utterly to subscribe to his conditions. The old man mildly strove to recall me to reason. Roused pride became the tyrant of my thought: I listened with indignation – I repelled him with disdain.

"Juliet, thou art mine! Did we not interchange vows in our innocent childhood? Are we not one in the sight of God? and shall thy cold-hearted, cold-blooded father divide us? Be generous, my love, be just; take not away a gift, last treasure of thy Guido – retract not thy vows – let us defy the world, and, setting at nought the calculations of age, find in our mutual affection a refuge from every ill."

Fiend I must have been with such sophistry to endeavour to poison that sanctuary of holy thought and tender love. Juliet shrank from me affrighted. Her father was the best and kindest of men, and she strove to show me how, in obeying him, every good would follow. He would receive my tardy submission with warm affection, and generous pardon would follow my repentance; – profitless words for a young and gentle daughter to use to a man accustomed to make his will law, and to feel in his own heart a despot so terrible and stern that he could yield obedience to nought save his own imperious desires!

My resentment grew with resistance; my wild companions were ready to add fuel to the flame. We laid a plan to carry off Juliet. At first it appeared to be crowned with success. Midway, on our return, we were overtaken by the agonized father and his attendants. A conflict ensued. Before the city guard came to decide the victory in favour of our antagonists, two of Torella's servitors were dangerously wounded.

This portion of my history weighs most heavily with me. Changed man as I am, I abhor myself in the recollection. May none who hear this tale ever have felt as I. A horse driven to fury by a rider armed with barbed spurs was not more a slave than I to the violent tyranny of my temper. A fiend possessed my soul, irritating it to madness. I felt the voice of conscience within me; but if I yielded to it for a brief interval, it was only to be a moment after torn, as by a whirlwind, away – borne along on the stream of desperate rage – the plaything of the storms engendered by pride. I was imprisoned, and, at the instance of Torella, set free. Again I returned to carry off both him and his child to France, which hapless country, then preyed on by freebooters and gangs of lawless soldiery, offered a grateful refuge to a criminal like me. Our plots were discovered. I was sentenced to banishment; and, as my debts were already enormous, my remaining property was put in the hands of commissioners for their payment. Torella again offered his mediation, requiring only my promise not to renew my abortive attempts on himself and his daughter. I spurned his offers, and fancied that I triumphed when I was thrust out from Genoa, a solitary and penniless exile. My companions were gone: they had been dismissed the city some weeks before, and were already in France. I was alone – friendless, with neither sword at my side, nor ducat in my purse.

I wandered along the sea-shore, a whirlwind of passion possessing and tearing my soul. It was as if a live coal had been set burning in my breast. At first I meditated on what *I should do*. I would join a band of freebooters. Revenge! – the word seemed balm to me; I hugged it, caressed it, till, like a serpent, it stung me. Then again I would abjure and despise Genoa, that little corner of the world. I would return to Paris, where so many of my friends swarmed; where my services would be eagerly accepted; where I would carve out fortune with my sword, and make my paltry birthplace and the false Torella rue the day when they drove me, a new Coriolanus, from her walls. I would return to Paris – thus on foot – a beggar – and present myself in my poverty to those I had formerly entertained sumptuously? There was gall in the mere thought of it.

The reality of things began to dawn upon my mind, bringing despair in its train. For several months I had been a prisoner: the evils of my dungeon had whipped my soul to madness, but they had subdued my corporeal frame. I was weak and wan. Torella had used a thousand artifices to administer to my comfort; I had detected and scorned them all, and I reaped the harvest of my obduracy. What was to be done? Should I crouch before my foe, and sue for forgiveness? – Die rather ten thousand deaths! – Never should they obtain that victory! Hate – I swore eternal hate! Hate from whom? – to whom? – From a wandering outcast – to a mighty noble! I and my feelings were nothing to them: already had they forgotten one so unworthy. And Juliet! – her angel face and sylph-like form gleamed among the clouds of my despair with vain beauty; for I had lost her – the glory and flower of the world! Another will call her his! – that smile of paradise will bless another!

Even now my heart fails within me when I recur to this rout of grim-visaged ideas. Now subdued almost to tears, now raving in my agony, still I wandered along the rocky shore, which grew at each step wilder and more desolate. Hanging rocks and hoar precipices overlooked the tideless ocean; black caverns yawned; and for ever, among the seaworn recesses, murmured and dashed the unfruitful waters. Now my way was almost barred by an abrupt promontory, now rendered nearly impracticable by fragments fallen from the cliff. Evening was at hand, when, seaward, arose, as if on the waving of a wizard's wand, a murky web of clouds, blotting the late azure sky, and darkening and disturbing the till now placid deep. The clouds had strange, fantastic shapes, and they changed and mingled and seemed to be driven about by a mighty spell. The waves raised their white crests; the thunder first muttered, then roared from across the waste of waters, which took a deep purple dye, flecked with foam. The spot where I stood looked, on one side, to the widespread ocean; on the other, it was barred by a rugged promontory. Round this cape suddenly came, driven by the wind, a vessel. In vain the mariners tried to force a path for her to the open sea – the gale drove her on the rocks. It will perish! – all on board will perish! Would I were among them! And to my young heart the idea of death came for the first time blended with that of joy. It was an awful sight to behold that vessel struggling with her fate. Hardly could I discern the sailors, but I heard them. It was soon all over! A rock, just covered by the tossing waves, and so unperceived, lay in wait for its prey. A crash of thunder broke over my head at the moment that, with a frightful shock, the vessel dashed upon her unseen enemy. In a brief space of time she went to pieces. There I stood in safety; and there were my fellow-creatures battling, how hopelessly, with annihilation. Methought I saw them struggling – too truly did I hear their shrieks, conquering the barking surges in their shrill agony. The dark breakers threw hither and thither the fragments of the wreck: soon it disappeared. I had been fascinated to gaze till the end: at last I sank on my knees – I covered my face with my hands. I again looked up; something was floating on the billows towards the shore. It neared and neared. Was that a human form? It grew more and more distinct; and at last a mighty wave, lifting the whole freight, lodged it upon a rock. A human being bestriding a sea-chest! – a human being! Yet was it one? Surely never such had existed before – a misshapen dwarf, with squinting eyes, distorted features, and body deformed, till it became a horror to behold. My blood, lately warming towards a fellow-being so snatched from a watery tomb, froze in my heart. The dwarf got off his chest; he tossed his straight, struggling hair from his odious visage.

"By St. Beelzebub!" he exclaimed, "I have been well bested." He looked round and saw me. "Oh, by the fiend! here is another ally of the mighty One. To what saint did you offer prayers, friend – if not to mine? Yet I remember you not on board."

I shrank from the monster and his blasphemy. Again he questioned me, and I muttered some inaudible reply. He continued:—

"Your voice is drowned by this dissonant roar. What a noise the big ocean makes! Schoolboys bursting from their prison are not louder than these waves set free to play. They disturb me. I will no more of their ill-timed brawling. Silence, hoary One! – Winds, avaunt! – to your homes! – Clouds, fly to the antipodes, and leave our heaven clear!"

As he spoke, he stretched out his two long, lank arms, that looked like spider's claws, and seemed to embrace with them the expanse before him. Was it a miracle? The clouds became broken and fled; the azure sky first peeped out, and then was spread a calm field of blue above us; the stormy gale was exchanged to the softly breathing west; the sea grew calm; the waves dwindled to riplets.

"I like obedience even in these stupid elements," said the dwarf. "How much more in the tameless mind of man! It was a well-got-up storm, you must allow – and all of my own making."

It was tempting Providence to interchange talk with this magician. But *Power*, in all its shapes, is respected by man. Awe, curiosity, a clinging fascination, drew me towards him.

"Come, don't be frightened, friend," said the wretch: "I am good-humoured when pleased; and something does please me in your well-proportioned body and handsome face, though you look a little woe-begone. You have suffered a land – I, a sea wreck. Perhaps I can allay the tempest of your fortunes as I did my own. Shall we be friends?" – And he held out his hand;

I could not touch it. "Well, then, companions – that will do as well. And now, while I rest after the buffeting I underwent just now, tell me why, young and gallant as you seem, you wander thus alone and downcast on this wild sea-shore."

The voice of the wretch was screeching and horrid, and his contortions as he spoke were frightful to behold. Yet he did gain a kind of influence over me, which I could not master, and I told him my tale. When it was ended, he laughed long and loud: the rocks echoed back the sound: hell seemed yelling around me.

"Oh, thou cousin of Lucifer!" said he; "so thou too hast fallen through thy pride; and, though bright as the son of Morning, thou art ready to give up thy good looks, thy bride, and thy well-being, rather than submit thee to the tyranny of good. I honour thy choice, by my soul! – So thou hast fled, and yield the day; and mean to starve on these rocks, and to let the birds peck out thy dead eyes, while thy enemy and thy betrothed rejoice in thy ruin. Thy pride is strangely akin to humility, methinks."

As he spoke, a thousand fanged thoughts stung me to the heart.

"What would you that I should do?" I cried.

"I! – Oh, nothing, but lie down and say your prayers before you die. But, were I you, I know the deed that should be done."

I drew near him. His supernatural powers made him an oracle in my eyes; yet a strange unearthly thrill quivered through my frame as I said, "Speak! – teach me – what act do you advise?"

"Revenge thyself, man! – humble thy enemies! – set thy foot on the old man's neck, and possess thyself of his daughter!"

"To the east and west I turn," cried I, "and see no means! Had I gold, much could I achieve; but, poor and single, I am powerless."

The dwarf had been seated on his chest as he listened to

my story. Now he got off; he touched a spring; it flew open! What a mine of wealth – of blazing jewels, beaming gold, and pale silver – was displayed therein. A mad desire to possess this treasure was born within me.

"Doubtless," I said, "one so powerful as you could do all things."

"Nay," said the monster humbly, "I am less omnipotent than I seem. Some things I possess which you may covet; but I would give them all for a small share, or even for a loan of what is yours."

"My possessions are at your service," I replied bitterly – "my poverty, my exile, my disgrace – I make a free gift of them all."

"Good! I thank you. Add one other thing to your gift, and my treasure is yours."

"As nothing is my sole inheritance, what besides nothing would you have?"

"Your comely face and well-made limbs."

I shivered. Would this all-powerful monster murder me? I had no dagger. I forgot to pray – but I grew pale.

"I ask for a loan, not a gift," said the frightful thing: "lend me your body for three days – you shall have mine to cage your soul the while, and, in payment, my chest. What say you to the bargain? – Three short days."

We are told that it is dangerous to hold unlawful talk; and well do I prove the same. Tamely written down, it may seem incredible that I should lend any ear to this proposition; but, in spite of his unnatural ugliness, there was something fascinating in a being whose voice could govern earth, air, and sea. I felt a keen desire to comply; for with that chest I could command the worlds. My only hesitation resulted from a fear that he would not be true to his bargain. Then, I thought, I shall soon die here on these lonely sands, and the limbs he covets will be mine no more: – it is worth the chance. And, besides, I knew that, by all the rules of art-magic, there were formula and oaths which none of its practisers dared break. I hesitated to reply; and he went on, now displaying his wealth, now speaking of the petty price he demanded, till it seemed madness to refuse. Thus is it; – place our bark in the current of the stream, and down, over fall and cataract it is hurried; give up our conduct to the wild torrent of passion, and we are away, we know not whither.

He swore many an oath, and I adjured him by many a sacred name; till I saw this wonder of power, this ruler of the elements, shiver like an autumn leaf before my words; and as if the spirit spake unwillingly and perforce within him, at last, he, with broken voice, revealed the spell whereby he might be obliged, did he wish to play me false, to render up the unlawful spoil. Our warm life-blood must mingle to make and to mar the charm.

Enough of this unholy theme. I was persuaded – the thing was done. The morrow dawned upon me as I lay upon the shingles, and I knew not my own shadow as it fell from me. I felt myself changed to a shape of horror, and cursed my easy faith and blind credulity. The chest was there – there the gold and precious stones for which I had sold the frame of flesh which nature had given me. The sight a little stilled my emotions: three days would soon be gone.

They did pass. The dwarf had supplied me with a plenteous store of food. At first I could hardly walk, so strange and out of joint were all my limbs; and my voice – it was that of the fiend. But I kept silent, and turned my face to the sun, that I might not see my shadow, and counted the hours, and ruminated on my future conduct. To bring Torella to my feet – to possess my Juliet in spite of him – all this my wealth could easily achieve. During dark night I slept, and dreamt of the accomplishment of my desires. Two suns had set – the third dawned. I was agitated, fearful. Oh expectation, what a frightful thing art thou, when kindled more by fear than hope! How dost thou twist thyself round the heart, torturing its pulsations! How dost thou dart unknown pangs all through our feeble mechanism, now seeming to shiver us like broken glass, to nothingness – now giving us a fresh strength, which can *do* nothing, and so torments us by a sensation, such as the strong man must feel who cannot break his fetters, though they bend in his grasp. Slowly paced the bright, bright orb up the eastern sky; long it lingered in the zenith, and still more slowly wandered down the west: it touched the horizon's verge – it was lost! Its glories were on the summits of the cliff – they grew dun and grey. The evening star shone bright. He will soon be here.

He came not! – By the living heavens, he came not! – and night dragged out its weary length, and, in its decaying age, "day began to grizzle its dark hair;" and the sun rose again on the most miserable wretch that ever upbraided its light. Three days thus I passed. The jewels and the gold – oh, how I abhorred them!

Well, well – I will not blacken these pages with demoniac ravings. All too terrible were the thoughts, the raging tumult of ideas that filled my soul. At the end of that time I slept; I had not before since the third sunset; and I dreamt that I was at Juliet's feet, and she smiled, and then she shrieked – for she saw my transformation – and again she smiled, for still her beautiful lover knelt before her. But it was not I – it was he, the fiend, arrayed in my limbs, speaking with my voice, winning her with my looks of love. I strove to warn her, but my tongue refused its office; I strove to tear him from her, but I was rooted to the ground – I awoke with the agony. There were the solitary hoar precipices – there the plashing sea, the quiet strand, and the blue sky over all. What did it mean? was my dream but a mirror of the truth? was he wooing and winning my betrothed? I would on the instant back to Genoa – but I was banished. I laughed – the dwarf's yell burst from my lips – *I* banished! Oh no! they had not exiled the foul limbs I wore; I might with these enter, without fear of incurring the threatened penalty of death, my own, my native city.

I began to walk towards Genoa. I was somewhat accustomed to my distorted limbs; none were ever so ill-adapted for a straightforward movement; it was with infinite difficulty that I proceeded. Then, too, I desired to avoid all the hamlets strewed here and there on the sea-beach, for I was unwilling to make a display of my hideousness. I was not quite sure that, if seen, the mere boys would not stone me to death as I passed, for a monster; some ungentle salutations I did receive from the few peasants or fishermen I chanced to meet. But it was dark night before I approached Genoa. The weather was so balmy and sweet that it struck me that the Marchese and his daughter would very probably have quitted the city for their country retreat. It was from Villa Torella that I had attempted to carry off Juliet; I had spent many an hour reconnoitring the spot, and knew each inch of ground in its vicinity. It was beautifully situated, embosomed in trees, on the margin of a stream. As I drew near, it became evident that my conjecture was right; nay, moreover, that the hours were being then devoted to feasting and merriment. For the house was lighted up; strains of soft and gay music were wafted towards me by the breeze. My heart sank within me. Such was the generous kindness of Torella's heart that I felt sure that he would not have indulged in public manifestations of rejoicing just after my unfortunate banishment, but for a cause I dared not dwell upon.

The country people were all alive and flocking about; it became necessary that I should conceal myself; and yet I longed to address some one, or to hear others discourse, or in any way to gain intelligence of what was really going on. At length, entering the walks that were in immediate vicinity to the mansion, I found one dark enough to veil my excessive frightfulness; and yet others as well as I were loitering in its shade. I soon gathered all I wanted to know – all that first made my very heart die with horror, and then boil with indignation. To-morrow Juliet was to be given to the penitent, reformed, beloved Guido – to-morrow my bride was to pledge her vows to a fiend from hell! And I did this! – my accursed pride – my demoniac violence and wicked self-idolatry had caused this act. For if I had acted as the wretch who had stolen my form had acted – if, with a mien at once yielding and dignified, I had presented myself to Torella, saying, I have done wrong, forgive me; I am unworthy of your angel-child, but permit me to claim her hereafter, when my altered conduct shall manifest that I abjure my vices, and endeavour to become in some sort worthy of her. I go to serve against the infidels; and when my zeal for religion and my true penitence for the past shall appear to you to cancel my crimes, permit me again to call myself your son. Thus had he spoken; and the penitent was welcomed even as the prodigal son of Scripture: the fatted calf was killed for him; and he, still pursuing the same path, displayed such open-hearted regret for his follies, so humble a concession of all his rights, and so ardent a resolve to reacquire them by a life of contrition and virtue, that he quickly conquered the kind old man; and full pardon, and the gift of his lovely child, followed in swift succession.

Oh, had an angel from Paradise whispered to me to act thus! But now, what would be the innocent Juliet's fate? Would God permit the foul union – or, some prodigy destroying it, link the dishonoured name of Carega with the worst of crimes? To-morrow at dawn they were to be married: there was but one way to prevent this – to meet mine enemy, and to enforce the ratification of our agreement. I felt that this could only be done by a mortal struggle. I had no sword – if indeed my distorted arms could wield a soldier's weapon – but I had a dagger, and in that lay my hope. There was no time for pondering or balancing nicely the question: I might die in the attempt; but besides the burning jealousy and despair of my own heart, honour, mere humanity, demanded that I should fall rather than not destroy the machinations of the fiend.

The guests departed – the lights began to disappear; it was evident that the inhabitants of the villa were seeking repose. I hid myself among the trees – the garden grew desert – the gates were closed – I wandered round and came under a window – ah! well did I know the same! – a soft twilight glimmered in the room – the curtains were half withdrawn. It was the temple of innocence and beauty. Its magnificence was tempered, as it were, by the slight disarrangements occasioned by its being dwelt in, and all the objects scattered around displayed the taste of her who hallowed it by her presence. I saw her enter with a quick light step – I saw her approach the window – she drew back the curtain yet further, and looked out into the night. Its breezy freshness played among her ringlets, and wafted them from the transparent marble of her brow. She clasped her hands, she raised her eyes to heaven. I heard her voice. Guido! she softly murmured – mine own Guido! and then, as if overcome by the fulness of her own heart, she sank on her knees; – her upraised eyes – her graceful attitude – the beaming thankfulness that lighted up her face – oh, these are tame words! Heart of mine, thou imagest ever, though thou canst not portray, the celestial beauty of that child of light and love.

I heard a step – a quick firm step along the shady avenue. Soon I saw a cavalier, richly dressed, young and, methought, graceful to look on, advance. I hid myself yet closer. The youth approached; he paused beneath the window. She arose, and again looking out she saw him, and said – I cannot, no, at this distant time I cannot record her terms of soft silver tenderness; to me they were spoken, but they were replied to by him.

"I will not go," he cried: "here where you have been, where your memory glides like some heaven-visiting ghost, I will pass the long hours till we meet, never, my Juliet, again, day or night, to part. But do thou, my love, retire; the cold morn and fitful breeze will make thy cheek pale, and fill with languor thy love-lighted eyes. Ah, sweetest! could I press one kiss upon them, I could, methinks, repose."

And then he approached still nearer, and methought he was about to clamber into her chamber. I had hesitated, not to terrify her; now I was no longer master of myself. I rushed forward – I threw myself on him – I tore him away – I cried, "O loathsome and foul-shaped wretch!"

I need not repeat epithets, all tending, as it appeared, to rail at a person I at present feel some partiality for. A shriek rose from Juliet's lips. I neither heard nor saw – I *felt* only mine enemy, whose throat I grasped, and my dagger's hilt; he struggled, but could not escape. At length hoarsely he breathed these words: "Do! – strike home! destroy this body – you will still live: may your life be long and merry!"

The descending dagger was arrested at the word, and he, feeling my hold relax, extricated himself and drew his sword, while the uproar in the house, and flying of torches from one room to the other, showed that soon we should be separated. In the midst of my frenzy there was much calculation: – fall I might, and so that he did not survive, I cared not for the death-blow I might deal against myself. While still, therefore, he thought I paused, and while I saw the villanous resolve to take advantage of my hesitation, in the sudden thrust he made at me, I threw myself on his sword, and at the same moment plunged my dagger, with a true, desperate aim, in his side. We fell together, rolling over each other, and the tide of blood that flowed from the gaping wound of each mingled on the grass. More I know not – I fainted.

Again I return to life: weak almost to death, I found myself stretched upon a bed – Juliet was kneeling beside it. Strange! my first broken request was for a mirror. I was so wan and ghastly, that my poor girl hesitated, as she told me afterwards; but, by the mass! I thought myself a right proper youth when I saw the dear reflection of my own well-known features. I confess it is a weakness, but I avow it, I do entertain a considerable affection for the countenance and limbs I behold, whenever I look at a glass; and have more mirrors in my house, and consult them oftener, than any beauty in Genoa. Before you too much condemn me, permit me to say that no one better knows than I the value of his own body; no one, probably, except myself, ever having had it stolen from him.

Incoherently I at first talked of the dwarf and his crimes, and reproached Juliet for her too easy admission of his love.

She thought me raving, as well she might; and yet it was some time before I could prevail on myself to admit that the Guido whose penitence had won her back for me was myself; and while I cursed bitterly the monstrous dwarf, and blest the well-directed blow that had deprived him of life, I suddenly checked myself when I heard her say, Amen! knowing that him whom she reviled was my very self. A little reflection taught me silence – a little practice enabled me to speak of that frightful night without any very excessive blunder. The wound I had given myself was no mockery of one – it was long before I recovered – and as the benevolent and generous Torella sat beside me, talking such wisdom as might win friends to repentance, and mine own dear Juliet hovered near me, administering to my wants, and cheering me by her smiles, the work of my bodily cure and mental reform went on together. I have never, indeed, wholly recovered my strength – my cheek is paler since – my person a little bent. Juliet sometimes ventures to allude bitterly to the malice that caused this change, but I kiss her on the moment, and tell her all is for the best. I am a fonder and more faithful husband, and true is this – but for that wound, never had I called her mine.

I did not revisit the sea-shore, nor seek for the fiend's treasure; yet, while I ponder on the past, I often think, and my confessor was not backward in favouring the idea, that it might be a good rather than an evil spirit, sent by my guardian angel, to show me the folly and misery of pride. So well at least did I learn this lesson, roughly taught as I was, that I am known now by all my friends and fellow-citizens by the name of Guido il Cortese.

THE EVIL EYE

"The wild Albanian kirtled to his knee,
With shawl-girt head, and ornamented gun,
And gold-embroider'd garments, fair to see;
The crimson-scarfed man of Macedon."

– LORD BYRON.

The Moreot, Katusthius Ziani, travelled wearily, and in fear of its robber-inhabitants, through the pashalik of Yannina; yet he had no cause for dread. Did he arrive, tired and hungry, in a solitary village, – did he find himself in the uninhabited wilds suddenly surrounded by a band of klephts, – or in the larger towns did he shrink at finding himself, sole of his race, among the savage mountaineers and despotic Turk, – as soon as he announced himself the Pobratimo[1] of Dmitri of the Evil Eye, every hand was held out, every voice spoke welcome.

The Albanian, Dmitri, was a native of the village of Korvo. Among the savage mountains of the district between Yannina and Terpellenè, the deep broad stream of Argyro-Castro flows; bastioned to the west by abrupt wood-covered precipices, shadowed to the east by elevated mountains. The highest

---

1. In Greece, especially in Illyria and Epirus, it is no uncommon thing for persons of the same sex to swear friendship. The Church contains a ritual to consecrate this vow. Two men thus united are called *pobratimi*, the women *posestrime*.

among these is Mount Trebucci; and in a romantic folding of that hill, distinct with minarets, crowned by a dome rising from out a group of pyramidal cypresses, is the picturesque village of Korvo. Sheep and goats form the apparent treasure of its inhabitants; their guns and yataghans, their warlike habits, and, with them, the noble profession of robbery, are sources of still greater wealth. Among a race renowned for dauntless courage and sanguinary enterprise, Dmitri was distinguished.

It was said that in his youth this klepht was remarkable for a gentler disposition and more refined taste than is usual with his countrymen. He had been a wanderer, and had learned European arts, of which he was not a little proud. He could read and write Greek, and a book was often stowed beside his pistols in his girdle. He had spent several years in Scio, the most civilised of the Greek islands, and had married a Sciote girl. The Albanians are characterized as despisers of women; but Dmitri, in becoming the husband of Helena, enlisted under a more chivalrous rule, and became the proselyte of a better creed. Often he returned to his native hills, and fought under the banner of the renowned Ali, and then came back to his island home. The love of the tamed barbarian was concentrated, burning, and something beyond this: it was a portion of his living, beating heart, – the nobler part of himself, – the diviner mould in which his rugged nature had been recast.

On his return from one of his Albanian expeditions he found his home ravaged by the Mainotes. Helena – they pointed to her tomb, nor dared tell him how she died; his only child, his lovely infant daughter, was stolen; his treasure-house of love and happiness was rifled, its gold-excelling wealth changed to blank desolation. Dmitri spent three years in endeavours to recover his lost offspring. He was exposed to a thousand dangers, underwent incredible hardships. He dared the wild beast in his lair, the Mainote in his port of refuge; he attacked, and was attacked by them. He wore the badge of his daring in a deep gash across his eyebrow and cheek. On this occasion he had died, but that Katusthius, seeing a scuffle on shore and a man left for dead, disembarked from a Moreot sacovela, carried him away, tended and cured him. They exchanged vows of friendship, and for some time the Albanian shared his brother's toils; but they were too pacific to suit his taste, and he returned to Korvo.

Who in the mutilated savage could recognise the handsomest amongst the Arnaoots? His habits kept pace with his change of physiognomy: he grew ferocious and hardhearted; he only smiled when engaged in dangerous enterprise. He had arrived at that worst state of ruffian feeling, the taking delight in blood. He grew old in these occupations; his mind became reckless, his countenance more dark; men trembled before his glance, women and children exclaimed in terror, "The Evil Eye!" The opinion became prevalent; he shared it himself; he gloried in the dread privilege; and when his victim shivered and withered beneath the mortal influence, the fiendish laugh with which he hailed this demonstration of his power struck with worse dismay the failing heart of the fascinated person. But Dmitri could command the arrows of his sight; and his comrades respected him the more for his supernatural attribute since they did not fear the exercise of it on themselves.

Dmitri had just returned from an expedition beyond Prevesa. He and his comrades were laden with spoil. They killed and roasted a goat whole for their repast; they drank dry several wine skins; then, round the fire in the court, they abandoned themselves to the delights of the kerchief dance, roaring out the chorus as they dropped upon and then rebounded from their knees, and whirled round and round with an activity all their own. The heart of Dmitri was heavy; he refused to dance, and sat apart, at first joining in the song with his voice and lute, till the air changed to one that reminded him of better days. His voice died away, his instrument dropped from his hands, and his head sank upon his breast.

At the sound of stranger footsteps he started up; in the form before him he surely recognised a friend – he was not mistaken. With a joyful exclamation he welcomed Katusthius

Ziani, clasping his hand and kissing him on the cheek. The traveller was weary, so they retired to Dmitri's own home, – a neatly plastered, white-washed cottage, whose earthen floor was perfectly dry and clean, and the walls hung with arms – some richly ornamented – and other trophies of his klephtic triumphs. A fire was kindled by his aged female attendant; the friends reposed on mats of white rushes while she prepared the pilaf and seethed flesh of kid. She placed a bright tin-tray on a block of wood before them, and heaped upon it cakes of Indian corn, goat's-milk cheese, eggs, and olives; a jar of water from their purest spring, and skin of wine, served to refresh and cheer the thirsty traveller.

After supper the guest spoke of the object of his visit.

"I come to my pobratimo," he said, "to claim the performance of his vow. When I rescued you from the savage Kakovougnis of Boularias, you pledged to me your gratitude and faith; do you disclaim the debt?"

Dmitri's brow darkened. "My brother," he cried, "need not remind me of what I owe. Command my life; in what can the mountain klepht aid the son of the wealthy Ziani!"

"The son of Ziani is a beggar," rejoined Katusthius, "and must perish if his brother deny his assistance."

The Moreot then told his tale. He had been brought up as the only son of a rich merchant of Corinth. He had often sailed as caravokeiri[2] of his father's vessels to Stamboul, and even to Calabria. Some years before he had been boarded and taken by a Barbary corsair. His life since then had been adventurous, he said; in truth, it had been a guilty one; – he had become a renegade, – and won regard from his new allies, not by his superior courage, for he was cowardly, but by the frauds that make men wealthy. In the midst of this career some superstition had influenced him, and he had returned to his ancient religion. He escaped from Africa, wandered through Syria, crossed to Europe, found occupation in Constantinople; and thus years passed. At last, as he was on the point of

---

2. Master of a merchant ship.

marriage with a Fanariote beauty, he fell again into poverty, and he returned to Corinth to see if his father's fortunes had prospered during his long wanderings. He found that while these had improved to a wonder, they were lost to him for ever. His father, during his protracted absence, acknowledged another son as his; and, dying a year before, had left all to him. Katusthius found this unknown kinsman, with his wife and child, in possession of his expected inheritance. Cyril divided with him, it is true, their parent's property, but Katusthius grasped at all, and resolved to obtain it. He brooded over a thousand schemes of murder and revenge; yet the blood of a brother was sacred to him, and Cyril, beloved and respected at Corinth, could only be attacked with considerable risk. Then his child was a fresh obstacle. As the best plan that presented itself, he hastily embarked for Butrinto, and came to claim the advice and assistance of the Arnaoot whose life he had saved, whose pobratimo he was. Not thus barely did he tell his tale, but glossed it over; so that had Dmitri needed the incitement of justice, which was not at all a desideratum with him, he would have been satisfied that Cyril was a base interloper, and that the whole transaction was one of imposture and villainy.

All night these men discussed a variety of projects, whose aim was, that the deceased Ziani's wealth should pass undivided into his elder son's hands. At morning's dawn Katusthius departed, and two days afterwards Dmitri quitted his mountain-home. His first care had been to purchase a horse, long coveted by him on account of its beauty and fleetness; he provided cartridges and replenished his powder-horn. His accoutrements were rich, his dress gay; his arms glittered in the sun. His long hair fell straight from under the shawl twisted round his cap, even to his waist; a shaggy white capote hung from his shoulder; his face wrinkled and puckered by exposure to the seasons; his brow furrowed with care; his mustachios long and jet-black; his scarred face; his wild, savage eyes; – his whole appearance, not deficient in barbaric grace, but stamped chiefly with ferocity and bandit pride, inspired, and we need not wonder, the superstitious Greek with a belief that a supernatural spirit of evil dwelt in his aspect, blasting and destroying. Now prepared for his journey, he departed from Korvo, crossing the woods of Acarnania, on his way to Morea.

"Wherefore does Zella tremble, and press her boy to her bosom, as if fearful of evil?" Thus asked Cyril Ziani, returning from the city of Corinth to his own rural abode. It was a home of beauty. The abruptly broken hills covered with olives, or brighter plantations of orange-trees, overlooked the blue waves of the Gulf of Egina. A myrtle underwood spread sweet scent around, and dipped its dark shining leaves into the sea itself. The low-roofed house was shaded by two enormous fig-trees, while vineyards and corn-land stretched along the gentle upland to the north. When Zella saw her husband she smiled, though her cheek was still pale and her lips quivering. "Now you are near to guard us," she said, "I dismiss fear; but danger threatens our Constans, and I shudder to remember that an Evil Eye has been upon him."

Cyril caught up his child. "By my head!" he cried, "thou speakest of an ill thing. The Franks call this superstition; but let us beware. His cheek is still rosy; his tresses flowing gold. Speak, Constans; hail thy father, my brave fellow!"

It was but a short-lived fear; no ill ensued, and they soon forgot an incident which had causelessly made their hearts to quail. A week afterwards Cyril returned, as he was wont, from shipping a cargo of currants, to his retreat on the coast. It was a beautiful summer evening: the creaking water-wheel, which produced the irrigation of the land, chimed in with the last song of the noisy cicala; the rippling waves spent themselves almost silently among the shingles. This was his home; but where its lovely flower? Zella did not come forth to welcome him. A domestic pointed to a chapel on a neighbouring acclivity, and there he found her; his child (nearly three years of age) was in his nurse's arms; his wife was praying fervently, while the tears streamed down her cheeks. Cyril demanded anxiously the meaning of this scene; but the nurse sobbed; Zella continued to pray and weep; and the boy, from sympathy, began to cry. This was too much for man to endure. Cyril left the chapel; he leant against a walnut-tree. His first exclamation was a customary Greek one, "Welcome this misfortune, so that it come single!" But what was the ill that had occurred? Unapparent was it yet; but the spirit of evil is most fatal when unseen. He was happy, – a lovely wife, a blooming child, a peaceful home, competence, and the prospect of wealth; these blessings were his: yet how often does Fortune use such as her decoys? He was a slave in an enslaved land, a mortal subject to the high destinies, and ten thousand were the envenomed darts which might be hurled at his devoted head. Now, timid and trembling, Zella came from the chapel: her explanation did not calm his fears. Again the Evil Eye had been on his child, and deep malignity lurked surely under this second visitation. The same man, an Arnaoot, with glittering arms, gay attire, mounted on a black steed, came from the neighbouring ilex grove, and, riding furiously up to the door, suddenly checked and reined in his horse at the very threshold. The child ran towards him: the Arnaoot bent his sinister eyes upon him: – "Lovely art thou, bright infant," he cried; "thy blue eyes are beaming, thy golden tresses fair to see; but thou art a vision fleeting as beautiful; – look at me!" The innocent looked up, uttered a shriek, and fell gasping on the ground. The women rushed forward to seize him; the Albanian put spurs to his horse, and, galloping swiftly across the little plain, up the wooded hill-side, he was soon lost to sight. Zella and the nurse bore the child to the chapel; they sprinkled him with holy water, and, as he revived, besought the Panagia with earnest prayers to save him from the menaced ill.

Several months elapsed; little Constans grew in intelligence and beauty; no blight had visited the flower of love, and its parents dismissed fear. Sometimes Cyril indulged in a joke at the expense of the Evil Eye; but Zella thought it unlucky to laugh, and crossed herself whenever the event was alluded to. At this time Katusthius visited their abode – "He was on his way," he said, "to Stamboul, and he came to know whether he could serve his brother in any of his transactions in the capital." Cyril and Zella received him with cordial affection: they rejoiced to perceive that fraternal love was beginning to warm his heart. He seemed full of ambition and hope: the brothers discussed his prospects, the politics of Europe, and the intrigues of the Fanar: the petty affairs of Corinth even were made subjects of discourse; and the probability that in a short time, young as he was, Cyril would be named Codja-Bashee of the province. On the morrow, Katusthius prepared to depart. "One favour does the voluntary exile ask – will my brother and sister accompany me some hours on my way to Napoli, whence I embark?"

Zella was unwilling to quit her home, even for a short interval; but she suffered herself to be persuaded, and they proceeded altogether for several miles towards the capital of the Morea. At noontide they made a repast under the shadow of a grove of oaks, and then separated. Returning homeward, the wedded pair congratulated themselves on their tranquil life and peaceful happiness, contrasted with the wanderer's lonely and homeless pleasures. These feelings increased in intensity as they drew nearer their dwelling, and anticipated the lisped welcome of their idolized child. From an eminence they looked upon the fertile vale which was their home: it was situated on the southern side of the isthmus, and looked upon the Gulf of Egina – all was verdant, tranquil, and beautiful. They descended into the plain; there a singular appearance attracted their attention. A plough with its yoke of oxen had been deserted midway in the furrow; the animals had dragged it to the side of the field, and endeavoured to repose as well as their conjunction permitted. The sun already touched its western bourne, and the summits of the trees were gilded by its parting beams. All was silent; even the eternal water-wheel was still; no menials appeared at their usual rustic labours. From the house the voice of wailing was too plainly heard. – "My child!" Zella exclaimed. Cyril began to reassure her; but another lament arose, and he hurried on. She dismounted, and would have followed him, but sank on the road-side. Her husband returned. "Courage, my beloved," he cried; "I will not repose night nor day until Constans is restored to us – trust to me – farewell!" With these words he rode swiftly on. Her worst fears were thus confirmed; her maternal heart, lately so joyous, became the abode of despair, while the nurse's narration of the sad occurrence tended but to add worse fear to fear. Thus it was: the same stranger of the Evil Eye had appeared, not as before, bearing down on them with eagle speed, but as if from a long journey; his horse lame and with drooping head; the Arnaoot himself covered with dust, apparently scarcely able to keep his seat. "By the life of your child," he said, "give a cup of water to one who faints with thirst." The nurse, with Constans in her arms, got a bowl of the desired liquid, and presented it. Ere the parched lips of the stranger touched the wave, the vessel fell from his hands. The woman started back, while he, at the same moment darting forward, tore with strong arm the child from her embrace. Already both were gone – with arrowy speed they traversed the plain, while her shrieks, and cries for assistance, called together all the domestics. They followed on the track of the ravisher, and none had yet returned. Now as night closed in, one by one they came back: they had nothing to relate; they had scoured the woods, crossed the hills – they could not even discover the route which the Albanian had taken.

On the following day Cyril returned, jaded, haggard, miserable; he had obtained no tidings of his son. On the morrow he again departed on his quest, nor came back for several days. Zella passed her time wearily – now sitting in hopeless despondency, now climbing the near hill to see whether she could perceive the approach of her husband. She was not allowed to remain long thus tranquil; the trembling domestics, left in guard, warned her that the savage forms of several Arnaoots had been seen prowling about: she herself saw a tall figure, clad in a shaggy white capote, steal round the promontory, and, on seeing her, shrink back: once at night the snorting and trampling of a horse roused her, not from slumber, but from her sense of security. Wretched as the bereft mother was, she felt personally almost reckless of danger; but she was not her own, she belonged to one beyond expression dear; and duty, as well as affection for him, enjoined self-preservation. Cyril, again returned: he was gloomier, sadder than before; but there was more resolution on his brow, more energy in his motions; he had obtained a clue, yet it might only lead him to the depths of despair.

He discovered that Katusthius had not embarked at Napoli. He had joined a band of Arnaoots lurking about Vasilico, and had proceeded to Patras with the Protoklepht; thence they put off together in a monoxylon for the northern shores of the Gulf of Lepanto: nor were they alone; they bore a child with them wrapt in a heavy torpid sleep. Poor Cyril's blood ran cold when he thought of the spells and witchcraft which had probably been put in practice on his boy. He would have followed close upon the robbers, but for the report that reached him that the remainder of the Albanians had proceeded southward towards Corinth. He could not enter upon a long wandering search among the pathless wilds of Epirus, leaving Zella exposed to the attacks of these bandits. He returned to consult with her, to devise some plan of action which would at once ensure her safety and promise success to his endeavours.

After some hesitation and discussion, it was decided that he should first conduct her to her native home, consult with her father as to his present enterprise, and be guided by his warlike experience before he rushed into the very focus of danger. The seizure of his child might only be a lure, and it were not well for him, sole protector of that child and its mother, to rush unadvisedly into the toils.

Zella, strange to say, for her blue eyes and brilliant complexion belied her birth, was the daughter of a Mainote: yet dreaded and abhorred by the rest of the world as are the inhabitants of Cape Tænarus, they are celebrated for their domestic virtues and the strength of their private attachments. Zella loved her father, and the memory of her rugged rocky home, from which she had been torn in an adverse hour. Near neighbours of the Mainotes, dwelling in the ruder and wildest portion of Maina, are the Kakovougnis, a dark suspicious race, of squat and stunted form, strongly contrasted with the tranquil cast of countenance characteristic of the Mainote. The two tribes are embroiled in perpetual quarrels; the narrow sea-girt abode which they share affords at once a secure place of refuge from the foreign enemy and all the facilities of internal mountain warfare. Cyril had once, during a coasting voyage, been driven by stress of weather into the little bay on whose shores is placed the small town of Kardamyla. The crew at first dreaded to be captured by the pirates; but they were reassured on finding them fully occupied by their domestic dissensions. A band of Kakovougnis were besieging the castellated rock overlooking Kardamyla, blockading the fortress in which the Mainote Capitano and his family had taken refuge. Two days passed thus, while furious contrary winds detained Cyril in the bay. On the third evening the western gale subsided, and a land-breeze promised to emancipate them from their perilous condition; when in the night, as they were about to put off in a boat from shore, they were hailed by a party of Mainotes, and one, an old man of commanding figure, demanded a parley. He was the Capitano of Kardamyla, the chief of the fortress, now attacked by his implacable enemies: he saw no escape – he must fall – and his chief desire was to save his treasure and his family from the hands of his enemies. Cyril consented to receive them on board: the latter consisted of an old mother, a paramana, and a young and beautiful girl, his daughter. Cyril conducted them in safety to Napoli. Soon after the Capitano's mother and paramana returned to their native town, while, with her father's consent, fair Zella became the wife of her preserver. The fortunes of the Mainote had prospered since then, and he stood first in rank, the chief of a large tribe, the Capitano of Kardamyla.

Thither then the hapless parents repaired; they embarked on board a small sacovela, which dropt down the Gulf of Egina, weathered the islands of Skyllo and Cerigo, and the extreme point of Tænarus: favoured by prosperous gales, they made the desired port, and arrived at the hospitable mansion of old Camaraz. He heard their tale with indignation; swore by his beard to dip his poniard in the best blood of Katusthius, and insisted upon accompanying his son-in-law on his expedition to Albania. No time was lost – the grey-headed mariner, still full of energy, hastened every preparation. Cyril and Zella parted; a thousand fears, a thousand hours of misery rose between the pair, late sharers in perfect happiness. The boisterous sea and distant lands were the smallest of the obstacles that divided them; they would not fear the worst; yet hope, a sickly plant, faded in their hearts as they tore themselves asunder after a last embrace.

Zella returned from the fertile district of Corinth to her barren native rocks. She felt all joy expire as she viewed from the rugged shore the lessening sails of the sacovela. Days and weeks passed, and still she remained in solitary and sad expectation: she never joined in the dance, nor made one in the assemblies of her countrywomen, who met together at eveningtide to sing, tell stories, and wile away the time in dance and gaiety. She secluded herself in the most lonely part of her father's house, and gazed unceasingly from the lattice upon the sea beneath, or wandered on the rocky beach; and when tempest darkened the sky, and each precipitous promontory grew purple under the shadows of the wide-winged clouds, when the roar of the surges was on the shore, and the white crests of the waves, seen afar upon the ocean-plain, showed like flocks of new-shorn sheep scattered along wide-extended downs, she felt neither gale nor inclement cold, nor returned home till recalled by her attendants. In obedience to them she sought the shelter of her abode, not to remain long; for the wild winds spoke to her, and the stormy ocean reproached her tranquillity. Unable to control the impulse, she would rush from her habitation on the cliff, nor remember, till she reached the shore, that her papooshes were left midway on the mountain-path, and that her forgotten veil and disordered dress were unmeet for such a scene. Often the unnumbered hours sped on, while this orphaned child of happiness leant on a cold dark rock; the low-browed crags beetled over her, the surges broke at her feet, her fair limbs were stained by spray, her tresses dishevelled by the gale. Hopelessly she wept until a sail appeared on the horizon; and then she dried her fast-flowing tears, fixing her large eyes upon the nearing hull or fading topsail. Meanwhile the storm tossed the clouds into a thousand gigantic shapes, and the tumultuous sea grew blacker and more wild; her natural gloom was heightened by superstitious horror; the Morai, the old Fates of her native Grecian soil, howled in the breezes; apparitions, which told of her child pining under the influence of the Evil Eye, and of her husband, the prey of some Thracian witchcraft, such as still is practised in the dread neighbourhood of Larissa, haunted her broken slumbers, and stalked like dire shadows across her waking thoughts. Her bloom was gone, her eyes lost their lustre, her limbs their round full beauty; her strength failed her, as she tottered to the accustomed spot to watch – vainly, yet for ever to watch.

What is there so fearful as the expectation of evil tidings delayed? Sometimes in the midst of tears, or worse, amidst the convulsive gaspings of despair, we reproach ourselves for influencing the eternal fates by our gloomy anticipations: then, if a smile wreathe the mourner's quivering lip, it is arrested by a throb of agony. Alas! are not the dark tresses of the young painted grey, the full cheek of beauty delved with sad lines by the spirits of such hours? Misery is a more welcome visitant when she comes in her darkest guise and wraps us in perpetual black, for then the heart no longer sickens with disappointed hope.

Cyril and old Camaraz had found great difficulty in doubling the many capes of the Morea as they made a coasting expedition from Kardamyla to the Gulf of Arta, north of Cefalonia and St. Mauro. During their voyage they had time to arrange their plans. As a number of Moreots travelling together might attract too much attention, they resolved to land their comrades at different points, and travel separately into the interior of Albania: Yannina was their first place of rendezvous. Cyril and his father-in-law disembarked in one of the most secluded of the many creeks which diversify the winding and precipitous shores of the gulf. Six others, chosen from the crew, would, by other routes, join them at the capital. They did not fear for themselves; alone, but well armed, and secure in the courage of despair, they penetrated the fastnesses of Epirus. No success cheered them: they arrived at Yannina without having made the slightest discovery. They were joined by their comrades, whom they directed to remain three days in the town, and then separately to proceed to Terpellenè, whither they immediately directed their steps. At the first village on their way thither, at "monastic Zitza," they obtained some information, not to direct, but to encourage their endeavours. They sought refreshment and hospitality in the monastery, which is situated on a green eminence, crowned by a grove of oak trees, immediately behind the village. Perhaps there is not in the world a more beautiful or more romantic spot, sheltered itself by clustering trees, looking out on one widespread landscape of hill and dale, enriched by vineyards, dotted with frequent flocks; while the Calamas in the depth of the vale gives life to the scene, and the far blue mountains of Zoumerkas, Sagori, Sulli, and Acroceraunia, to the east, west, north, and south, close in the various prospects. Cyril half envied the Caloyers their inert tranquillity. They received the travellers gladly, and were cordial though simple in their manners. When questioned concerning the object of their journey, they warmly sympathized with the father's anxiety, and eagerly told all they knew. Two weeks before, an Arnaoot, well known to them as Dmitri of the Evil Eye, a famous klepht of Korvo, and a Moreot, arrived, bringing with them a child, – a bold, spirited, beautiful boy, who, with firmness beyond his years, claimed the protection of the Caloyers, and accused his companions of having carried him off by force from his parents.

"By my head!" cried the Albanian, "a brave Palikar: he keeps his word, brother; he swore by the Panagia, in spite of our threats of throwing him down a precipice, food for the vulture, to accuse us to the first good men he saw: he neither pines under the Evil Eye, nor quails beneath our menaces."

Katusthius frowned at these praises, and it became evident during their stay at the monastery that the Albanian and the Moreot quarrelled as to the disposal of the child. The rugged mountaineer threw off all his sternness as he gazed upon the boy. When little Constans slept, he hung over him, fanning away with woman's care the flies and gnats. When he spoke, he answered with expressions of fondness, winning him with gifts, teaching him, all child as he was, a mimicry of warlike exercises. When the boy knelt and besought the Panagia to restore him to his parents, his voice quivering, and tears running down his cheeks, the eyes of Dmitri overflowed; he cast his cloak over his face; his heart whispered to him: "Thus, perhaps, my child prayed. Heaven was deaf. Alas! where is she now?"

Encouraged by such signs of compassion, which children are quick to perceive, Constans twined his arms round his neck, telling him that he loved him, and that he would fight for him when a man, if he would take him back to Corinth. At such words Dmitri would rush forth, seek Katusthius, remonstrate with him, till the unrelenting man checked him by reminding him of his vow. Still he swore that no hair of the child's head should be injured; while the uncle, unvisited by compunction, meditated his destruction. The quarrels which thence arose were frequent, and violent, till Katusthius, weary of opposition, had recourse to craft to obtain his purpose. One night he secretly left the monastery, bearing the child with him. When Dmitri heard of his evasion, it was a fearful thing to the good Caloyers only to look upon him; they instinctively clutched hold of every bit of iron on which they could lay their hands, so to avert the Evil Eye which glared with native and untamed fierceness. In their panic a whole score of them had rushed to the iron-plated door which led out of their abode: with the strength of a lion, Dmitri tore them away, threw back the portal, and, with the swiftness of a torrent fed by the thawing of the snows in spring, he dashed down the steep hill – the flight of an eagle not more rapid; the course of a wild beast not more resolved.

Such was the clue afforded to Cyril. It were too long to follow him in his subsequent search; he, with old Camaraz, wandered through the vale of Argyro-Castro, and climbed Mount Trebucci to Korvo. Dmitri had returned; he had gathered together a score of faithful comrades, and sallied forth again; various were the reports of his destination, and the enterprise which he meditated. One of these led our adventurers to Terpellenè, and hence back towards Yannina; and now chance again favoured them. They rested one night in the habitation of a priest at the little village of Mosme, about three leagues to the north of Zitza; and here they found an Arnaoot who had been disabled by a fall from his horse; this man was to have made one of Dmitri's band: they learned from him that the Arnaoot had tracked Katusthius, following him close, and forcing him to take refuge in the monastery of the Prophet Elias, which stands on an elevated peak of the mountains of Sagori, eight leagues from Yannina. Dmitri had followed him, and demanded the child. The Caloyers refused to give it up, and the klepht, roused to mad indignation, was now besieging and battering the monastery, to obtain by force this object of his newly-awakened affections.

At Yannina, Camaraz and Cyril collected their comrades,

and departed to join their unconscious ally. He, more impetuous than a mountain stream or ocean's fiercest waves, struck terror into the hearts of the recluses by his ceaseless and dauntless attacks. To encourage them to further resistance, Katusthius, leaving the child behind in the monastery, departed for the nearest town of Sagori, to entreat its Belouk-Bashee to come to their aid. The Sagorians are a mild, amiable, social people; they are gay, frank, clever; their bravery is universally acknowledged, even by the more uncivilised mountaineers of Zoumerkas; yet robbery, murder, and other acts of violence are unknown among them. These good people were not a little indignant when they heard that a band of Arnaoots was besieging and battering the sacred retreat of their favourite Caloyers. They assembled in a gallant troop, and, taking Katusthius with them, hastened to drive the insolent klephts back to their ruder fastnesses. They came too late. At midnight, while the monks prayed fervently to be delivered from their enemies, Dmitri and his followers tore down their iron-plated door and entered the holy precincts. The Protoklepht strode up to the gates of the sanctuary, and, placing his hands upon it, swore that he came to save, not to destroy. Constans saw him. With a cry of delight he disengaged himself from the Caloyer who held him, and rushed into his arms: this was sufficient triumph. With assurance of sincere regret for having disturbed them, the klepht quitted the chapel with his followers, taking his prize with him.

Katusthius returned some hours after, and so well did the traitor plead his cause with the kind Sagorians, bewailing the fate of his little nephew among those evil men, that they offered to follow, and, superior as their numbers were, to rescue the boy from their destructive hands. Katusthius, delighted with the proposition, urged their immediate departure. At dawn they began to climb the mountain summits, already trodden by the Zoumerkians.

Delighted with repossessing his little favourite, Dmitri placed him before him on his horse, and, followed by his comrades, made his way over the mountains, clothed with old Dodona's oaks, or, in higher summits, by dark gigantic pines. They proceeded for some hours, and at length dismounted to repose. The spot they chose was the depth of a dark ravine, whose gloom was increased by the broad shadows of dark ilexes; an entangled underwood, and a sprinkling of craggy isolated rocks, made it difficult for the horses to keep their footing. They dismounted, and sat by the little stream. Their simple fare was spread, and Dmitri enticed the boy to eat by a thousand caresses. Suddenly one of his men, set as a guard, brought intelligence that a troop of Sagorians, with Katusthius as their guide, was advancing from the monastery of St. Elias; while another man gave the alarm of the approach of six or eight well-armed Moreots, who were advancing on the road from Yannina; in a moment every sign of encampment had disappeared. The Arnaoots began to climb the hills, getting under cover of the rocks, and behind the large trunks of the forest trees, keeping concealed till their invaders should be in the very midst of them. Soon the Moreots appeared, turning round the defile, in a path that only allowed them to proceed two by two; they were unaware of danger, and walked carelessly, until a shot that whizzed over the head of one, striking the bough of a tree, recalled them from their security. The Greeks, accustomed to the same mode of warfare, betook themselves also to the safeguards of the rocks, firing from behind them, striving with their adversaries which should get to the most elevated station; jumping from crag to crag, and dropping down and firing as quickly as they could load: one old man alone remained on the pathway. The mariner, Camaraz, had often encountered the enemy on the deck of his caick, and would still have rushed foremost at a boarding, but this warfare required too much activity. Cyril called on him to shelter himself beneath a low, broad stone: the Mainote waved his hand. "Fear not for me," he cried; "I know how to die!"

The brave love the brave. Dmitri saw the old man stand,

unflinching, a mark for all the balls, and he started from behind his rocky screen, calling on his men to cease. Then addressing his enemy, he cried, "Who art thou? Wherefore art thou here? If ye come in peace, proceed on your way. Answer, and fear not!"

The old man drew himself up, saying, "I am a Mainote, and cannot fear. All Hellas trembles before the pirates of Cape Matapan, and I am one of these! I do not come in peace! Behold! you have in your arms the cause of our dissension! I am the grandsire of that child – give him to me!"

Dmitri, had he held a snake which he felt awakening in his bosom, could not so suddenly have changed his cheer; – "the offspring of a Mainote!" – he relaxed his grasp; – Constans would have fallen had he not clung to his neck. Meanwhile each party had descended from their rocky station, and were grouped together in the pathway below. Dmitri tore the child from his neck – he felt as if he could, with savage delight, dash him down the precipice; when, as he paused and trembled from excess of passion, Katusthius, and the foremost Sagorians, came down upon them.

"Stand!" cried the infuriated Arnaoot. "Behold, Katusthius! behold, friend, whom I, driven by the resistless fates, madly and wickedly forswore! I now perform thy wish – the Mainote child dies! the son of the accursed race shall be the victim of my just revenge!"

Cyril, in a transport of fear, rushed up the rock; he levelled his musket but he feared to sacrifice his child. The old Mainote, less timid and more desperate, took a steady aim; Dmitri saw the act, and hurled the dagger, already raised against the child, at him, – it entered his side, – while Constans, feeling his late protector's grasp relax, sprang from it into his father's arms.

Camaraz had fallen, yet his wound was slight. He saw the Arnaoots and Sagorians close round him; he saw his own followers made prisoners. Dmitri and Katusthius had both thrown themselves upon Cyril, struggling to repossess themselves of the screaming boy. The Mainote raised himself – he was feeble of limb, but his heart was strong; he threw himself before the father and child; he caught the upraised arm of Dmitri. "On me," he cried, "fall all thy vengeance! I of the evil race! for the child, he is innocent of such parentage! Maina cannot boast him for a son!"

"Man of lies!" commenced the infuriated Arnaoot, "this falsehood shall not stead thee!"

"Nay, by the souls of those you have loved, listen!" continued Camaraz, "and if I make not good my words, may I and my children die! The boy's father is a Corinthian, his mother, a Sciote girl!"

"Scio!" the very word made the blood recede to Dmitri's heart. "Villain!" he cried, dashing aside Katusthius' arm, which was raised against poor Constans, "I guard this child – dare not to injure him! Speak, old man, and fear not, so that thou speakest the truth."

"Fifteen years ago," said Camaraz, "I hovered with my caick, in search of prey, on the coast of Scio. A cottage stood on the borders of a chestnut wood; it was the habitation of the widow of a wealthy islander – she dwelt in it with her only daughter, married to an Albanian, then absent; – the good woman was reported to have a concealed treasure in her house – the girl herself would be rich spoil – it was an adventure worth the risk. We ran our vessel up a shady creek, and, on the going down of the moon, landed; stealing under the covert of night towards the lonely abode of these women."

Dmitri grasped at his dagger's hilt – it was no longer there; he half drew a pistol from his girdle – little Constans, again confiding in his former friend, stretched out his hands and clung to his arm; the klepht looked on him, half yielded to his desire to embrace him, half feared to be deceived; so he turned away, throwing his capote over his face, veiling his anguish, controlling his emotions, till all should be told. Camaraz continued:

"It became a worse tragedy than I had contemplated. The

girl had a child – she feared for its life, and struggled with the men like a tigress defending her young. I was in another room seeking for the hidden store, when a piercing shriek rent the air – I never knew what compassion was before – this cry went to my heart; but it was too late, the poor girl had sunk to the ground, the life-tide oozing from her bosom. I know not why, but I turned woman in my regret for the slain beauty. I meant to have carried her and her child on board, to see if aught could be done to save her, but she died ere we left the shore. I thought she would like her island grave best, and truly feared that she might turn vampire to haunt me, did I carry her away; so we left her corpse for the priests to bury, and carried off the child, then about two years old. She could say few words except her own name – that was Zella, and she is the mother of this boy!"

A succession of arrivals in the bay of Kardamyla had kept poor Zella watching for many nights. Her attendant had, in despair of ever seeing her sleep again, drugged with opium the few cakes she persuaded her to eat, but the poor woman did not calculate on the power of mind over body, of love over every enemy, physical or moral, arrayed against it. Zella lay on her couch, her spirit somewhat subdued, but her heart alive, her eyes unclosed. In the night, led by some unexplained impulse, she crawled to her lattice, and saw a little sacovela enter the bay; it ran in swiftly, under favour of the wind, and was lost to her sight under a jutting crag. Lightly she trod the marble floor of her chamber; she drew a large shawl close round her; she descended the rocky pathway, and reached, with swift steps, the beach – still the vessel was invisible, and she was half inclined to think that it was the offspring of her excited imagination – yet she lingered. She felt a sickness at her very heart whenever she attempted to move, and her eye-lids weighed down in spite of herself. The desire of sleep at last became irresistible; she lay down on the shingles, reposed her head on the cold, hard pillow, folded her shawl still closer, and gave herself up to forgetfulness.

So profoundly did she slumber under the influence of the opiate, that for many hours she was insensible of any change in her situation. By degrees only she awoke, by degrees only became aware of the objects around her; the breeze felt fresh and free – so was it ever on the wave-beaten coast; the waters rippled near, their dash had been in her ears as she yielded to repose; but this was not her stony couch, that canopy, not the dark overhanging cliff. Suddenly she lifted up her head – she was on the deck of a small vessel, which was skimming swiftly over the ocean-waves – a cloak of sables pillowed her head; the shores of Cape Matapan were to her left, and they steered right towards the noonday sun. Wonder rather than fear possessed her: with a quick hand she drew aside the sail that veiled her from the crew – the dreaded Albanian was sitting close at her side, her Constans cradled in his arms; she uttered a cry – Cyril turned at the sound, and in a moment she was folded in his embrace.

Ferdinando Eboli

During this quiet time of peace we are fast forgetting the exciting and astonishing events of the Napoleonic wars; and the very names of Europe's conquerors are becoming antiquated to the ears of our children. Those were more romantic days than these; for the revulsions occasioned by revolution or invasion were full of romance; and travellers in those countries in which these scenes had place hear strange and wonderful stories, whose truth so much resembles fiction, that, while interested in the narration, we never give implicit credence to the narrator. Of this kind is a tale I heard at Naples. The fortunes of war perhaps did not influence its actors, yet it appears improbable that any circumstances so out of the usual routine could have had place under the garish daylight that peace sheds upon the world.

When Murat, then called Gioacchino, king of Naples, raised his Italian regiments, several young nobles, who had before been scarcely more than vine-dressers on the soil, were inspired with a love of arms, and presented themselves as candidates for military honours. Among these was the young Count Eboli. The father of this youthful noble had followed Ferdinand to Sicily; but his estates lay principally near Salerno, and he was naturally desirous of preserving them; while the hopes that the French government held out of glory and prosperity to his country made him often regret that he had followed his legitimate but imbecile king to exile. When he died, therefore, he recommended his son to return to Naples, to present himself to his old and tried friend, the Marchese Spina, who held a high office in Murat's government, and through his means to reconcile himself to the new king. All this was easily achieved. The young and gallant Count was permitted to possess his patrimony; and, as a further pledge of good fortune, he was betrothed to the only child of the Marchese Spina. The nuptials were deferred till the end of the ensuing campaign.

Meanwhile the army was put in motion, and Count Eboli only obtained such short leave of absence as permitted him to visit for a few hours the villa of his future father-in-law, there to take leave of him and his affianced bride. The villa was situated on one of the Apennines to the north of Salerno, and looked down, over the plain of Calabria, in which Pæstum is situated, on to the blue Mediterranean. A precipice on one side, a brawling mountain torrent, and a thick grove of ilex, added beauty to the sublimity of its site. Count Eboli ascended the mountain-path in all the joy of youth and hope. His stay was brief. An exhortation and a blessing from the Marchese, a tender farewell, graced by gentle tears, from the fair Adalinda, were the recollections he was to bear with him, to inspire him with courage and hope in danger and absence. The sun had just sunk behind the distant isle of Istria, when, kissing his lady's hand, he said a last "Addio," and with slower steps, and more melancholy mien, rode down the mountain on his road to Naples.

That same night Adalinda retired early to her apartment, dismissing her attendants; and then, restless from mingled fear and hope, she threw open the glass-door that led to a balcony looking over the edge of the hill upon the torrent, whose loud rushing often lulled her to sleep, but whose waters were concealed from sight by the ilex trees, which lifted their topmost branches above the guarding parapet of the balcony.

Leaning her cheek upon her hand, she thought of the

dangers her lover would encounter, of her loneliness the while, of his letters, and of his return. A rustling sound now caught her ear. Was it the breeze among the ilex trees? Her own veil was unwaved by every wind, her tresses even, heavy in their own rich beauty only, were not lifted from her cheek. Again those sounds. Her blood retreated to her heart, and her limbs trembled. What could it mean? Suddenly the upper branches of the nearest tree were disturbed; they opened, and the faint starlight showed a man's figure among them. He prepared to spring from his hold on to the wall. It was a feat of peril. First the soft voice of her lover bade her "Fear not," and on the next instant he was at her side, calming her terrors, and recalling her spirits, that almost left her gentle frame, from mingled surprise, dread, and joy. He encircled her waist with his arm, and pouring forth a thousand passionate expressions of love, she leant on his shoulder, and wept from agitation, while he covered her hands with kisses, and gazed on her with ardent adoration.

Then in calmer mood they sat together; triumph and joy lighted up his eyes, and a modest blush glowed on her cheek: for never before had she sat alone with him, nor heard unrestrained his impassioned assurances of affection. It was, indeed, Love's own hour. The stars trembled on the roof of his eternal temple; the dashing of the torrent, the mild summer atmosphere, and the mysterious aspect of the darkened scenery, were all in unison to inspire security and voluptuous hope. They talked of how their hearts, through the medium of divine nature, might hold commune during absence; of the joys of reunion, and of their prospect of perfect happiness.

The moment at last arrived when he must depart. "One tress of this silken hair," said he, raising one of the many curls that clustered on her neck. "I will place it on my heart, a shield to protect me against the swords and balls of the enemy." He drew his keen-edged dagger from its sheath. "Ill weapon for so gentle a deed," he said, severing the lock, and at the same moment many drops of blood fell fast on the fair arm of the lady. He answered her fearful inquiries by showing a gash he had awkwardly inflicted on his left hand. First he insisted on securing his prize, and then he permitted her to bind his wound, which she did half laughing, half in sorrow, winding round his hand a riband loosened from her own arm. "Now, farewell," he cried; "I must ride twenty miles ere dawn, and the descending Bear shows that midnight is past." His descent was difficult, but he achieved it happily, and the stave of a song – whose soft sounds rose like the smoke of incense from an altar – from the dell below, to her impatient ear, assured her of his safety.

As is always the case when an account is gathered from eye-witnesses, I never could ascertain the exact date of these events. They occurred, however, while Murat was king of Naples; and when he raised his Italian regiments, Count Eboli, as aforesaid, became a junior officer in them, and served with much distinction, though I cannot name either the country or the battle in which he acted so conspicuous a part that he was on the spot promoted to a troop.

Not long after this event, and while he was stationed in the north of Italy, Gioacchino, sending for him to headquarters late one evening, entrusted him with a confidential mission, across a country occupied by the enemy's troops, to a town possessed by the French. It was necessary to undertake the expedition during the night, and he was expected to return on that succeeding the following day. The king himself gave him his despatches and the word; and the noble youth, with modest firmness, protested that he would succeed, or die, in the fulfilment of his trust.

It was already night, and the crescent moon was low in the west, when Count Ferdinando Eboli, mounting his favourite horse, at a quick gallop cleared the streets of the town; and then, following the directions given him, crossed the country among the fields planted with vines, carefully avoiding the main road. It was a beauteous and still night; calm and sleep occupied the earth; war, the blood-hound, slumbered; the spirit of love alone had life at that silent hour. Exulting in the hope of glory, our young hero commenced his journey, and visions of aggrandizement and love formed his reveries. A distant sound roused him: he checked his horse and listened; voices approached. When recognising the speech of a German, he turned from the path he was following, to a still straighter way. But again the tone of an enemy was heard, and the trampling of horses. Eboli did not hesitate; he dismounted, tied his steed to a tree, and, skirting along the enclosure of the field, trusted to escape thus unobserved. He succeeded after an hour's painful progress, and arrived on the borders of a stream, which, as the boundary between two states, was the mark of his having finally escaped danger. Descending the steep bank of the river, which, with his horse, he might perhaps have forded, he now prepared to swim. He held his despatch in one hand, threw away his cloak, and was about to plunge into the water, when from under the dark shade of the *argine*, which had concealed them, he was suddenly arrested by unseen hands, cast on the ground, bound, gagged, and blinded, and then placed into a little boat, which was sculled with infinite rapidity down the stream.

There seemed so much of premeditation in the act that it baffled conjecture, yet he must believe himself a prisoner to the Austrian. While, however, he still vainly reflected, the boat was moored, he was lifted out, and the change of atmosphere made him aware that they entered some house. With extreme care and celerity, yet in the utmost silence, he was stripped of his clothes, and two rings he wore drawn from his fingers; other habiliments were thrown over him; and then no departing footstep was audible; but soon he heard the splash of a single oar, and he felt himself alone. He lay perfectly unable to move, the only relief his captor or captors had afforded him being the exchange of the gag for a tightly-bound handkerchief. For hours he thus remained, with a tortured mind, bursting with rage, impatience, and disappointment; now writhing as well as he could in his endeavours to free himself, now still in despair.

His despatches were taken away, and the period was swiftly passing when he could by his presence have remedied in some degree this evil. The morning dawned, and, though the full glare of the sun could not visit his eyes, he felt it play upon his limbs. As the day advanced, hunger preyed on him, and, though amidst the visitation of mightier, he at first disdained this minor, evil, towards evening it became, in spite of himself, the predominant sensation. Night approached, and the fear that he should remain, and even starve, in this unvisited solitude had more than once thrilled through his frame, when feminine voices and a child's gay laugh met his ear. He heard persons enter the apartment, and he was asked in his native language, while the ligature was taken from his mouth, the cause of his present situation. He attributed it to banditti. His bonds were quickly cut, and his banded eyes restored to sight. It was long before he recovered himself. Water brought from the stream, however, was some refreshment, and by degrees he resumed the use of his senses, and saw that he was in a dilapidated shepherd's cot, with no one near him save the peasant girl and a child, who had liberated him. They rubbed his ankles and wrists, and the little fellow offered him some bread and eggs, after which refreshment and an hour's repose Ferdinando felt himself sufficiently restored to revolve his adventure in his mind, and to determine on the conduct he was to pursue.

He looked at the dress which had been given him in exchange for that which he had worn. It was of the plainest and meanest description. Still no time was to be lost; and he felt assured that the only step he could take was to return with all speed to the headquarters of the Neapolitan army, and inform the king of his disasters and his loss.

It were long to follow his backward steps, and to tell all of indignation and disappointment that swelled his heart. He walked painfully but resolutely all night, and by three in the morning entered the town where Gioacchino then was. He was challenged by the sentinels; he gave the word confided to him by Murat, and was instantly made prisoner by the soldiers. He declared to them his name and rank, and the necessity he was under of immediately seeing the king. He was taken to the guard-house, and the officer on duty there listened with contempt to his representations, telling him that Count Ferdinando Eboli had returned three hours before, ordering him to be confined for further examination as a spy. Eboli loudly insisted that some impostor had taken his name; and while he related the story of his capture, another officer came in, who recognised his person; other individuals acquainted with him joined the party; and as the impostor had been seen by none but the officer of the night, his tale gained ground.

A young Frenchman of superior rank, who had orders to attend the king early in the morning, carried a report of what was going forward to Murat himself. The tale was so strange that the king sent for the young Count; and then, in spite of having seen and believed in his counterfeit a few hours before, and having received from him an account of his mission, which had been faithfully executed, the appearance of the youth staggered him, and he commanded the presence of him who, as Count Eboli, had appeared before him a few hours previously. As Ferdinand stood beside the king, his eye glanced at a large and splendid mirror. His matted hair, his bloodshot eyes, his haggard looks, and torn and mean dress, derogated from the nobility of his appearance; and still less did he appear like the magnificent Count Eboli, when, to his utter confusion and astonishment, his counterfeit stood beside him.

He was perfect in all the outward signs that denoted high birth; and so like him whom he represented, that it would have been impossible to discern one from the other apart. The same chestnut hair clustered on his brow; the sweet and animated hazel eyes were the same; the one voice was the echo of the other. The composure and dignity of the pretender gained the suffrages of those around. When he was told of the strange appearance of another Count Eboli, he laughed in a frank good-humoured manner, and, turning to Ferdinand, said, "You honour me much in selecting me for your personation; but there are two or three things I like about myself so well, that you must excuse my unwillingness to exchange myself for you." Ferdinand would have answered, but the false Count, with greater haughtiness, turning to the king, said, "Will your majesty decide between us? I cannot bandy words with a fellow of this sort." Irritated by scorn, Ferdinand demanded leave to challenge the pretender; who said, that if the king and his brother-officers did not think that he should degrade himself and disgrace the army by going out with a common vagabond, he was willing to chastise him, even at the peril of his own life. But the king, after a few more questions, feeling assured that the unhappy noble was an impostor, in severe and menacing terms reprehended him for his insolence, telling him that he owed it to his mercy alone that he was not executed as a spy, ordering him instantly to be conducted without the walls of the town, with threats of weighty punishment if he ever dared to subject his impostures to further trial.

It requires a strong imagination, and the experience of much misery, fully to enter into Ferdinand's feelings. From high rank, glory, hope, and love, he was hurled to utter beggary and disgrace. The insulting words of his triumphant rival, and the degrading menaces of his so lately gracious sovereign, rang in his ears; every nerve in his frame writhed with agony. But, fortunately for the endurance of human life, the worst misery in early youth is often but a painful dream, which we cast off when slumber quits our eyes. After a struggle with intolerable anguish, hope and courage revived in his heart. His resolution was quickly made. He would return to Naples, relate his story to the Marchese Spina, and through his influence obtain at least an impartial hearing from the king. It was not, however, in his peculiar situation, an easy task to put his determination into effect. He was penniless; his dress bespoke poverty; he had neither friend nor kinsman near, but such as would behold in him the most impudent of swindlers. Still his courage did not fail him. The kind Italian soil, in the autumnal season now advanced, furnished him with chestnuts, arbutus berries, and grapes. He took the most direct road over the hills, avoiding towns, and indeed every habitation; travelling principally in the night, when, except in cities, the officers of government had retired from their stations. How he succeeded in getting from one end of Italy to the other it is difficult to say; but certain it is, that, after the interval of a few weeks, he presented himself at the Villa Spina.

With considerable difficulty he obtained admission to the presence of the Marchese, who received him standing, with an inquiring look, not at all recognising the noble youth. Ferdinand requested a private interview, for there were several visitors present. His voice startled the Marchese, who complied, taking him into another apartment. Here Ferdinand disclosed himself, and, with rapid and agitated utterance, was relating the history of his misfortunes, when the tramp of horses was heard, the great bell rang, and a domestic announced "Count Ferdinando Eboli." "It is himself," cried the youth, turning pale. The words were strange, and they appeared still more so when the person announced entered; the perfect semblance of the young noble, whose name he assumed, as he had appeared when last at his departure, he trod the pavement of the hall. He inclined his head gracefully to the baron, turning with a glance of some surprise, but more disdain, towards Ferdinand, exclaiming, "Thou here!"

Ferdinand drew himself up to his full height. In spite of fatigue, ill-fare, and coarse garments, his manner was full of dignity. The Marchese looked at him fixedly, and started as he marked his proud mien, and saw in his expressive features the very face of Eboli. But again he was perplexed when he turned and discerned, as in a mirror, the same countenance reflected by the new-comer, who underwent this scrutiny somewhat impatiently. In brief and scornful words he told the Marchese that this was a second attempt in the intruder to impose himself as Count Eboli; that the trick had failed before, and would again; adding, laughing, that it was hard to be brought to prove himself to be himself, against the assertion of a *briccone*, whose likeness to him, and matchless impudence, were his whole stock-in-trade.

"Why, my good fellow," continued he, sneeringly, "you put me out of conceit with myself, to think that one, apparently so like me, should get on no better in the world."

The blood mounted into Ferdinand's cheeks on his enemy's bitter taunts; with difficulty he restrained himself from closing with his foe, while the words "traitorous impostor!" burst from his lips. The baron commanded the fierce youth to be silent, and, moved by a look that he remembered to be Ferdinand's, he said gently, "By your respect for me, I adjure you to be patient; fear not but that I will deal impartially." Then turning to the pretended Eboli, he added that he could not doubt but that he was the true Count, and asked excuse for his previous indecision. At first the latter appeared angry, but at length he burst into a laugh, and then, apologising for his ill-breeding, continued laughing heartily at the perplexity of the Marchese. It is certain his gaiety gained more credit with his auditor than the indignant glances of poor Ferdinand. The false Count then said that, after the king's menaces, he had entertained no expectation that the farce was to be played over again. He had obtained leave of absence, of which he profited to visit his future father-in-law, after having spent a few days in his own palazzo at Naples. Until now Ferdinand had listened silently, with a feeling of curiosity, anxious to learn all he could of the actions and motives of his rival; but at these last words he could no longer contain himself.

"What!" cried he, "hast thou usurped my place in my own father's house, and dared assume my power in my ancestral halls?"

A gush of tears overpowered the youth; he hid his face in his hands. Fierceness and pride lit up the countenance of the pretender.

57

"By the eternal God and the sacred cross, I swear," he exclaimed, "that palace is my father's palace; those halls the halls of my ancestors!"

Ferdinand looked up with surprise: "And the earth opens not," he said, "to swallow the perjured man."

He then, at the call of the Marchese, related his adventures, while scorn mantled on the features of his rival. The Marchese, looking at both, could not free himself from doubt. He turned from one to the other: in spite of the wild and disordered appearance of poor Ferdinand, there was something in him that forbade his friend to condemn him as the impostor; but then it was utterly impossible to pronounce such the gallant and noble-looking youth, who could only be acknowledged as the real Count by the disbelief of the other's tale. The Marchese, calling an attendant, sent for his fair daughter.

"This decision," said he, "shall be made over to the subtle judgment of a woman, and the keen penetration of one who loves."

Both the youths now smiled – the same smile; the same expression – that of anticipated triumph. The baron was more perplexed than ever.

Adalinda had heard of the arrival of Count Eboli, and entered, resplendent in youth and happiness. She turned quickly towards him who resembled most the person she expected to see; when a well-known voice pronounced her name, and she gazed aghast on the double appearance of the lover. Her father, taking her hand, briefly explained the mystery, and bade her assure herself which was her affianced husband.

"Signorina," said Ferdinand, "disdain me not because I appear before you thus in disgrace and misery. Your love, your goodness will restore me to prosperity and happiness."

"I know not by what means," said the wondering girl, "but surely you are Count Eboli."

"Adalinda," said the rival youth, "waste not your words on

a villain. Lovely and deceived one, I trust, trembling I say it, that I can with one word assure you that I am Eboli."

"Adalinda," said Ferdinand, "I placed the nuptial ring on your finger; before God your vows were given to me."

The false Count approached the lady, and, bending one knee, took from his heart a locket, enclosing hair tied with a green riband, which she recognised to have worn, and pointed to a slight scar on his left hand.

Adalinda blushed deeply, and, turning to her father, said, motioning towards the kneeling youth,—

"He is Ferdinand."

All protestations now from the unhappy Eboli were vain. The Marchese would have cast him into a dungeon; but at the earnest request of his rival, he was not detained, but thrust ignominiously from the villa. The rage of a wild beast newly chained was less than the tempest of indignation that now filled the heart of Ferdinand. Physical suffering, from the fatigue and fasting, was added to his internal anguish; for some hours madness, if that were madness which never forgets its ill, possessed him. In a tumult of feelings there was one predominant idea: it was to take possession of his father's house, and to try, by ameliorating the fortuitous circumstances of his lot, to gain the upper hand of his adversary. He expended his remaining strength in reaching Naples, entered his family palace, and was received and acknowledged by his astonished domestics.

One of his first acts was to take from a cabinet a miniature of his father encircled with jewels, and to invoke the aid of the paternal spirit. Refreshment and a bath restored him to some of his usual strength; and he looked forward with almost childish delight to one night to be spent in peace under the roof of his father's house. This was not permitted. Ere midnight the great bell sounded: his rival entered as master, with the Marchese Spina. The result may be divined. The Marchese appeared more indignant than the false Eboli. He insisted that the unfortunate youth should be imprisoned. The portrait, whose setting was costly, found on him, proved him guilty of robbery. He was given into the hands of the police, and thrown into a dungeon. I will not dwell on the subsequent scenes. He was tried by the tribunal, condemned as guilty, and sentenced to the galleys for life.

On the eve of the day when he was to be removed from the Neapolitan prison to work on the roads in Calabria, his rival visited him in his dungeon. For some moments both looked at the other in silence. The impostor gazed on the prisoner with mingled pride and compassion: there was evidently a struggle in his heart. The answering glance of Ferdinand was calm, free, and dignified. He was not resigned to his hard fate, but he disdained to make any exhibition of despair to his cruel and successful foe. A spasm of pain seemed to wrench the bosom of the false one; and he turned aside, striving to recover the hardness of heart which had hitherto supported him in the prosecution of his guilty enterprise. Ferdinand spoke first.

"What would the triumphant criminal with his innocent victim?"

His visitant replied haughtily, "Do not address such epithets to me, or I leave you to your fate: I am that which I say I am."

"To me this boast!" cried Ferdinand scornfully; "but perhaps these walls have ears."

"Heaven, at least, is not deaf," said the deceiver; "favouring Heaven, which knows and admits my claim. But a truce to this idle discussion. Compassion – a distaste to see one so very like myself in such ill condition – a foolish whim, perhaps, on which you may congratulate yourself – has led me hither. The bolts of your dungeon are drawn; here is a purse of gold; fulfil one easy condition, and you are free."

"And that condition?"

"Sign this paper."

He gave to Ferdinand a writing, containing a confession of his imputed crimes. The hand of the guilty youth trembled as he gave it; there was confusion in his mien, and a restless uneasy rolling of his eye. Ferdinand wished in one mighty word, potent as lightning, loud as thunder, to convey his burning disdain of this proposal: but expression is weak, and calm is more full of power than storm. Without a word, he tore the paper in two pieces and threw them at the feet of his enemy.

With a sudden change of manner, his visitant conjured him, in voluble and impetuous terms, to comply. Ferdinand answered only by requesting to be left alone. Now and then a half word broke uncontrollably from his lips; but he curbed himself. Yet he could not hide his agitation when, as an argument to make him yield, the false Count assured him that he was already married to Adalinda. Bitter agony thrilled poor Ferdinand's frame; but he preserved a calm mien, and an unaltered resolution. Having exhausted every menace and every persuasion, his rival left him, the purpose for which he came unaccomplished. On the morrow, with many others, the refuse of mankind, Count Ferdinando Eboli was led in chains to the unwholesome plains of Calabria, to work there at the roads.

I must hurry over some of the subsequent events, for a detailed account of them would fill volumes. The assertion of the usurper of Ferdinand's right, that he was already married to Adalinda, was, like all else he said, false. The day was, however, fixed for their union, when the illness and the subsequent death of the Marchese Spina delayed its celebration. Adalinda retired during the first months of mourning to a castle belonging to her father not far from Arpino, a town of the kingdom of Naples, in the midst of the Apennines, about 50 miles from the capital. Before she went, the deceiver tried to persuade her to consent to a private marriage. He was probably afraid that, in the long interval that was about to ensue before he could secure her, she would discover his imposture. Besides, a rumour had gone abroad that one of the fellow-prisoners of Ferdinand, a noted bandit, had escaped, and that the young count was his companion in flight. Adalinda, however, refused to comply with her lover's entreaties, and retired to her seclusion with an old aunt, who was blind and deaf, but an excellent duenna. The false Eboli seldom visited his mistress; but he was a master in his art, and subsequent events showed that he must have spent all his time, disguised, in the vicinity of the castle. He contrived by various means, unsuspected at the moment, to have all Adalinda's servants changed for creatures of his own; so that, without her being aware of the restraint, she was, in fact, a prisoner in her own house. It is impossible to say what first awakened her suspicions concerning the deception put upon her. She was an Italian, with all the habitual quiescence and lassitude of her countrywomen in the ordinary routine of life, and with all their energy and passion when roused. The moment the doubt darted into her mind she resolved to be assured. A few questions relative to scenes that had passed between poor Ferdinand and herself sufficed for this. They were asked so suddenly and pointedly that the pretender was thrown off his guard; he looked confused, and stammered in his replies. Their eyes met; he felt that he was detected, and she saw that he perceived her now confirmed suspicions. A look such as is peculiar to an impostor – a glance that deformed his beauty, and filled his usually noble countenance with the hideous lines of cunning and cruel triumph – completed her faith in her own discernment. "How," she thought, "could I have mistaken this man for my own gentle Eboli?" Again their eyes met. The peculiar expression of his terrified her, and she hastily quitted the apartment.

Her resolution was quickly formed. It was of no use to attempt to explain her situation to her old aunt. She determined to depart immediately for Naples, throw herself at the feet of Gioacchino, and to relate and obtain credit for her strange history. But the time was already lost when she could have executed this design. The contrivances of the deceiver were complete – she found herself a prisoner. Excess of fear gave her boldness, if not courage. She sought her jailor. A few minutes before she had been a young and thoughtless girl, docile as a child, and as unsuspecting; now she felt as if she had suddenly grown old in wisdom, and that the experience of years had been gained in that of a few seconds.

During their interview she was wary and firm, while the instinctive power of innocence over guilt gave majesty to her demeanour. The contriver of her ills for a moment cowered beneath her eye. At first he would by no means allow that he was not the person he pretended to be, but the energy and eloquence of truth bore down his artifice, so that, at length driven into a corner, he turned – a stag at bay. Then it was her turn to quail, for the superior energy of a man gave him the mastery. He declared the truth: he was the elder brother of Ferdinand, a natural son of the old Count Eboli. His mother, who had been wronged, never forgave her injurer, and bred her son in deadly hate for his parent, and a belief that the advantages enjoyed by his more fortunate brother were rightfully his own. His education was rude; but he had an Italian's subtle talents, swiftness of perception, and guileful arts.

"It would blanch your cheek," he said to his trembling auditress, "could I describe all that I have suffered to achieve my purpose. I would trust to none – I executed all myself. It was a glorious triumph, but due to my perseverance and my fortitude, when I and my usurping brother stood – I, the noble, he, the degraded outcast – before our sovereign."

Having rapidly detailed his history, he now sought to win the favourable ear of Adalinda, who stood with averted and angry looks. He tried by the varied shows of passion and tenderness to move her heart. Was he not, in truth, the object of her love? Was it not he who scaled her balcony at Villa Spina? He recalled scenes of mutual overflow of feeling to her mind, thus urging arguments the most potent with a delicate woman. Pure blushes tinged her cheek, but horror of the deceiver predominated over every other sentiment. He swore that as soon as they should be united he would free

Ferdinand, and bestow competency, nay, if so she willed it, half his possessions on him. She coldly replied, that she would rather share the chains of the innocent, and misery, than link herself with imposture and crime. She demanded her liberty; but the untamed and even ferocious nature that had borne the deceiver through his career of crime now broke forth, and he invoked fearful imprecations on his head if she ever quitted the castle except as his wife. His look of conscious power and unbridled wickedness terrified her; her flashing eyes spoke abhorrence. It would have been far easier for her to have died than have yielded the smallest point to a man who had made her feel for one moment his irresistible power, arising from her being an unprotected woman, wholly in his hands. She left him, feeling as if she had just escaped from the impending sword of an assassin.

One hour's deliberation suggested to her a method of escape from her terrible situation. In a wardrobe at the castle lay, in their pristine gloss, the habiliments of a page of her mother, who had died suddenly, leaving these unworn relics of his station. Dressing herself in these, she tied up her dark shining hair, and even, with a somewhat bitter feeling, girded on the slight sword that appertained to the costume. Then, through a private passage leading from her own apartment to the chapel of the castle, she glided with noiseless steps, long after the Ave Maria, sounded at four o'clock, had, on a November night, given token that half an hour had passed since the setting of the sun. She possessed the key of the chapel door – it opened at her touch; she closed it behind her, and she was free. The pathless hills were around her, the starry heavens above, and a cold wintry breeze murmured around the castle walls; but fear of her enemy conquered every other fear, and she tripped lightly on in a kind of ecstasy for many a long hour over the stony mountain path – she, who had never before walked more than a mile or two from home at any time in her life – till her feet were blistered, her slight shoes cut through, her way utterly lost. At morning's dawn she found herself in the midst of the wild ilex-covered Apennines, and neither habitation nor human being apparent.

She was hungry and weary. She had brought gold and jewels with her; but here were no means of exchanging these for food. She remembered stories of banditti, but none could be so ruffian-like and cruel as him from whom she fled. This thought, a little rest, and a draught of water from a pure mountain-spring, restored her to some portion of courage, and she continued her journey. Noonday approached; and, in the south of Italy, the noonday sun, when unclouded, even in November, is oppressively warm, especially to an Italian woman, who never exposes herself to its beams. Faintness came over her. There appeared recesses in the mountain sides along which she was travelling, grown over with bay and arbutus: she entered one of these, there to repose. It was deep, and led to another that opened into a spacious cavern lighted from above: there were cates, grapes, and a flagon of wine on a rough-hewn table. She looked fearfully around, but no inhabitant appeared. She placed herself at the table, and, half in dread, ate of the food presented to her; and then sat, her elbow on the table, her head resting on her little snow-white hand, her dark hair shading her brow and clustering round her throat. An appearance of languor and fatigue was diffused through her attitude, while her soft black eyes filled at intervals with large tears as, pitying herself, she recurred to the cruel circumstances of her lot. Her fanciful but elegant dress, her feminine form, her beauty and her grace, as she sat pensive and alone in the rough unhewn cavern, formed a picture a poet would describe with delight, an artist love to paint.

"She seemed a being of another world; a seraph, all light and beauty: a Ganymede, escaped from his thrall above to his natal Ida. It was long before I recognised, looking down on her from the opening hill, my lost Adalinda." Thus spoke the young Count Eboli, when he related this story; for its end was as romantic as its commencement.

When Ferdinando had arrived, a galley-slave in Calabria,

he found himself coupled with a bandit, a brave fellow, who abhorred his chains, from love of freedom, as much as his fellow-prisoner did, from all the combination of disgrace and misery they brought upon him. Together they devised a plan of escape, and succeeded in effecting it. On their road, Ferdinand related his story to the outlaw, who encouraged him to hope for a favourable turn of fate; and meanwhile invited and persuaded the desperate man to share his fortunes as a robber among the wild hills of Calabria.

The cavern where Adalinda had taken refuge was one of their fastnesses, whither they betook themselves at periods of imminent danger for safety only, as no booty could be collected in that unpeopled solitude; and there, one afternoon, returning from the chase, they found the wandering, fearful, solitary, fugitive girl; and never was lighthouse more welcome to tempest-tossed sailor than was her own Ferdinand to his lady-love.

Fortune, now tired of persecuting the young noble, favoured him still further. The story of the lovers interested the bandit chief, and promise of reward secured him. Ferdinand persuaded Adalinda to remain one night in the cave, and on the following morning they prepared to proceed to Naples; but at the moment of their departure they were surprised by an unexpected visitant: the robbers brought in a prisoner – it was the impostor. Missing on the morrow her who was the pledge of his safety and success, but assured that she could not have wandered far, he despatched emissaries in all directions to seek her; and himself, joining in the pursuit, followed the road she had taken, and was captured by these lawless men, who expected rich ransom from one whose appearance denoted rank and wealth. When they discovered who their prisoner was, they generously delivered him up into his brother's hands.

Ferdinand and Adalinda proceeded to Naples. On their arrival, she presented herself to Queen Caroline; and, through her, Murat heard with astonishment the device that had been practised on him. The young Count was restored to his honours and possessions, and within a few months afterwards was united to his betrothed bride.

The compassionate nature of the Count and Countess led them to interest themselves warmly in the fate of Ludovico, whose subsequent career was more honourable but less fortunate. At the intercession of his relative, Gioacchino permitted him to enter the army, where he distinguished himself, and obtained promotion. The brothers were at Moscow together, and mutually assisted each other during the horrors of the retreat. At one time overcome by drowsiness, the mortal symptom resulting from excessive cold, Ferdinand lingered behind his comrades; but Ludovico, refusing to leave him, dragged him on in spite of himself, till, entering a village, food and fire restored him, and his life was saved. On another evening, when wind and sleet added to the horror of their situation, Ludovico, after many ineffective struggles, slid from his horse lifeless; Ferdinand was at his side, and, dismounting, endeavoured by every means in his power to bring back pulsation to his stagnant blood. His comrades went forward, and the young Count was left alone with his dying brother in the white boundless waste. Once Ludovico opened his eyes and recognised him; he pressed his hand, and his lips moved to utter a blessing as he died. At that moment the welcome sounds of the enemy's approach roused Ferdinand from the despair into which his dreadful situation plunged him. He was taken prisoner, and his life was thus saved. When Napoleon went to Elba, he, with many others of his countrymen, was liberated, and returned to Naples.

THE MORTAL IMMORTAL

July 16, 1833. – This is a memorable anniversary for me; on it I complete my three hundred and twenty-third year!

The Wandering Jew? – certainly not. More than eighteen centuries have passed over his head. In comparison with him, I am a very young Immortal.

Am I, then, immortal? This is a question which I have asked myself, by day and night, for now three hundred and three years, and yet cannot answer it. I detected a grey hair amidst my brown locks this very day – that surely signifies decay. Yet it may have remained concealed there for three hundred years – for some persons have become entirely white-headed before twenty years of age.

I will tell my story, and my reader shall judge for me. I will tell my story, and so contrive to pass some few hours of a long eternity, become so wearisome to me. For ever! Can it be? to live for ever! I have heard of enchantments, in which the victims were plunged into a deep sleep, to wake, after a hundred years, as fresh as ever: I have heard of the Seven Sleepers – thus to be immortal would not be so burthensome: but, oh! the weight of never-ending time – the tedious passage of the still-succeeding hours! How happy was the fabled Nourjahad! – But to my task.

All the world has heard of Cornelius Agrippa. His memory is as immortal as his arts have made me. All the world has also heard of his scholar, who, unawares, raised the foul fiend during his master's absence, and was destroyed by him. The report, true or false, of this accident, was attended with many inconveniences to the renowned philosopher. All his scholars at once deserted him – his servants disappeared. He had no one near him to put coals on his ever-burning fires while he slept, or to attend to the changeful colours of his medicines while he studied. Experiment after experiment failed, because one pair of hands was insufficient to complete them: the dark spirits laughed at him for not being able to retain a single mortal in his service.

I was then very young – very poor – and very much in love. I had been for about a year the pupil of Cornelius, though I was absent when this accident took place. On my return, my friends implored me not to return to the alchymist's abode. I trembled as I listened to the dire tale they told; I required no second warning; and when Cornelius came and offered me a purse of gold if I would remain under his roof, I felt as if Satan himself tempted me. My teeth chattered – my hair stood on end; – I ran off as fast as my trembling knees would permit.

My failing steps were directed whither for two years they had every evening been attracted, – a gently bubbling spring of pure living water, beside which lingered a dark-haired girl, whose beaming eyes were fixed on the path I was accustomed each night to tread. I cannot remember the hour when I did not love Bertha; we had been neighbours and playmates from infancy, – her parents, like mine, were of humble life, yet respectable, – our attachment had been a source of pleasure to them. In an evil hour, a malignant fever carried off both her father and mother, and Bertha became an orphan. She would have found a home beneath my paternal roof, but, unfortunately, the old lady of the near castle, rich, childless, and solitary, declared her intention to adopt her. Henceforth Bertha was clad in silk – inhabited a marble palace – and was looked on as being highly favoured by fortune. But in her new situation among her new associates, Bertha remained true to the friend of her humbler days; she often visited the cottage of my father, and when forbidden to go thither, she would stray towards the neighbouring wood, and meet me beside its shady fountain.

She often declared that she owed no duty to her new protectress equal in sanctity to that which bound us. Yet still I was too poor to marry, and she grew weary of being tormented on my account. She had a haughty but an impatient spirit, and grew angry at the obstacles that prevented our union. We met now after an absence, and she had been sorely beset while I was away; she complained bitterly, and almost reproached me for being poor. I replied hastily,—

"I am honest, if I am poor! – were I not, I might soon become rich!"

This exclamation produced a thousand questions. I feared to shock her by owning the truth, but she drew it from me; and then, casting a look of disdain on me, she said,—

"You pretend to love, and you fear to face the Devil for my sake!"

I protested that I had only dreaded to offend her; – while she dwelt on the magnitude of the reward that I should receive. Thus encouraged – shamed by her – led on by love and hope, laughing at my late fears, with quick steps and a light heart, I returned to accept the offers of the alchymist, and was instantly installed in my office.

A year passed away. I became possessed of no insignificant sum of money. Custom had banished my fears. In spite of the most painful vigilance, I had never detected the trace of a cloven foot; nor was the studious silence of our abode ever disturbed by demoniac howls. I still continued my stolen interviews with Bertha, and Hope dawned on me – Hope – but not perfect joy; for Bertha fancied that love and security were enemies, and her pleasure was to divide them in my bosom. Though true of heart, she was somewhat of a coquette in manner; and I was jealous as a Turk. She slighted me in a thousand ways, yet would never acknowledge herself to be in the wrong. She would drive me mad with anger, and then force me to beg her pardon. Sometimes she fancied that I was not sufficiently submissive, and then she had some story of a rival, favoured by her protectress. She was surrounded by silk-clad youths – the rich and gay. What chance had the sad-robed scholar of Cornelius compared with these?

On one occasion, the philosopher made such large demands upon my time, that I was unable to meet her as I was wont. He was engaged in some mighty work, and I was forced to remain, day and night, feeding his furnaces and watching his chemical preparations. Bertha waited for me in vain at the fountain. Her haughty spirit fired at this neglect; and when at last I stole out during the few short minutes allotted to me for slumber, and hoped to be consoled by her, she received me with disdain, dismissed me in scorn, and vowed that any man should possess her hand rather than he who could not be in two places at once for her sake. She would be revenged! And truly she was. In my dingy retreat I heard that she had been hunting, attended by Albert Hoffer. Albert Hoffer was favoured by her protectress; and the three passed in cavalcade before my smoky window. Methought that they mentioned my name; it was followed by a laugh of derision, as her dark eyes glanced contemptuously towards my abode.

Jealousy, with all its venom and all its misery, entered my breast. Now I shed a torrent of tears, to think that I should never call her mine; and, anon, I imprecated a thousand curses on her inconstancy. Yet, still I must stir the fires of the alchymist, still attend on the changes of his unintelligible medicines.

Cornelius had watched for three days and nights, nor closed his eyes. The progress of his alembics was slower than he expected: in spite of his anxiety, sleep weighed upon his eyelids. Again and again he threw off drowsiness with more than human energy; again and again it stole away his senses. He eyed his crucibles wistfully. "Not ready yet," he murmured; "will another night pass before the work is accomplished?

Winzy, you are vigilant – you are faithful – you have slept, my boy – you slept last night. Look at that glass vessel. The liquid it contains is of a soft rose-colour: the moment it begins to change its hue, awaken me – till then I may close my eyes. First, it will turn white, and then emit golden flashes; but wait not till then; when the rose-colour fades, rouse me." I scarcely heard the last words, muttered, as they were, in sleep. Even then he did not quite yield to nature. "Winzy, my boy," he again said, "do not touch the vessel – do not put it to your lips; it is a philter – a philter to cure love; you would not cease to love your Bertha – beware to drink!"

And he slept. His venerable head sunk on his breast, and I scarce heard his regular breathing. For a few minutes I watched the vessel – the rosy hue of the liquid remained unchanged. Then my thoughts wandered – they visited the fountain, and dwelt on a thousand charming scenes never to be renewed – never! Serpents and adders were in my heart as the word "Never!" half formed itself on my lips. False girl! – false and cruel! Never more would she smile on me as that evening she smiled on Albert. Worthless, detested woman! I would not remain unrevenged – she should see Albert expire at her feet – she should die beneath my vengeance. She had smiled in disdain and triumph – she knew my wretchedness and her power. Yet what power had she? – the power of exciting my hate – my utter scorn – my – oh, all but indifference! Could I attain that – could I regard her with careless eyes, transferring my rejected love to one fairer and more true, that were indeed a victory!

A bright flash darted before my eyes. I had forgotten the medicine of the adept; I gazed on it with wonder: flashes of admirable beauty, more bright than those which the diamond emits when the sun's rays are on it, glanced from the surface of the liquid; an odour the most fragrant and grateful stole over my sense; the vessel seemed one globe of living radiance, lovely to the eye, and most inviting to the taste. The first thought, instinctively inspired by the grosser sense, was, I will

– I must drink. I raised the vessel to my lips. "It will cure me of love – of torture!" Already I had quaffed half of the most delicious liquor ever tasted by the palate of man, when the philosopher stirred. I started – I dropped the glass – the fluid flamed and glanced along the floor, while I felt Cornelius's gripe at my throat, as he shrieked aloud, "Wretch! you have destroyed the labour of my life!"

The philosopher was totally unaware that I had drunk any portion of his drug. His idea was, and I gave a tacit assent to it, that I had raised the vessel from curiosity, and that, frighted at its brightness, and the flashes of intense light it gave forth, I had let it fall. I never undeceived him. The fire of the medicine was quenched – the fragrance died away – he grew calm, as a philosopher should under the heaviest trials, and dismissed me to rest.

I will not attempt to describe the sleep of glory and bliss which bathed my soul in paradise during the remaining hours of that memorable night. Words would be faint and shallow types of my enjoyment, or of the gladness that possessed my bosom when I woke. I trod air – my thoughts were in heaven. Earth appeared heaven, and my inheritance upon it was to be one trance of delight. "This it is to be cured of love," I thought; "I will see Bertha this day, and she will find her lover cold and regardless; too happy to be disdainful, yet how utterly indifferent to her!"

The hours danced away. The philosopher, secure that he had once succeeded, and believing that he might again, began to concoct the same medicine once more. He was shut up with his books and drugs, and I had a holiday. I dressed myself with care; I looked in an old but polished shield, which served me for a mirror; methought my good looks had wonderfully improved. I hurried beyond the precincts of the town, joy in my soul, the beauty of heaven and earth around me. I turned my steps towards the castle – I could look on its lofty turrets with lightness of heart, for I was cured of love. My Bertha saw me afar off, as I came up the avenue. I know not what sudden impulse animated her bosom, but at the sight, she sprung with a light fawn-like bound down the marble steps, and was hastening towards me. But I had been perceived by another person. The old high-born hag, who called herself her protectress, and was her tyrant, had seen me also; she hobbled, panting, up the terrace; a page, as ugly as herself, held up her train, and fanned her as she hurried along, and stopped my fair girl with a "How, now, my bold mistress? whither so fast? Back to your cage – hawks are abroad!"

Bertha clasped her hands – her eyes were still bent on my approaching figure. I saw the contest. How I abhorred the old crone who checked the kind impulses of my Bertha's softening heart. Hitherto, respect for her rank had caused me to avoid the lady of the castle; now I disdained such trivial considerations. I was cured of love, and lifted above all human fears; I hastened forwards, and soon reached the terrace. How lovely Bertha looked! her eyes flashing fire, her cheeks glowing with impatience and anger, she was a thousand times more graceful and charming than ever. I no longer loved – Oh no! I adored – worshipped – idolized her!

She had that morning been persecuted, with more than usual vehemence, to consent to an immediate marriage with my rival. She was reproached with the encouragement that she had shown him – she was threatened with being turned out of doors with disgrace and shame. Her proud spirit rose in arms at the threat; but when she remembered the scorn that she had heaped upon me, and how, perhaps, she had thus lost one whom she now regarded as her only friend, she wept with remorse and rage. At that moment I appeared. "Oh, Winzy!" she exclaimed, "take me to your mother's cot; swiftly let me leave the detested luxuries and wretchedness of this noble dwelling – take me to poverty and happiness."

I clasped her in my arms with transport. The old dame was speechless with fury, and broke forth into invective only when we were far on our road to my natal cottage. My mother received the fair fugitive, escaped from a gilt cage to nature and liberty, with tenderness and joy; my father, who loved her, welcomed her heartily; it was a day of rejoicing, which did not need the addition of the celestial potion of the alchymist to steep me in delight.

Soon after this eventful day, I became the husband of Bertha. I ceased to be the scholar of Cornelius, but I continued his friend. I always felt grateful to him for having, unawares, procured me that delicious draught of a divine elixir, which, instead of curing me of love (sad cure! solitary and joyless remedy for evils which seem blessings to the memory), had inspired me with courage and resolution, thus winning for me an inestimable treasure in my Bertha.

I often called to mind that period of trance-like inebriation with wonder. The drink of Cornelius had not fulfilled the task for which he affirmed that it had been prepared, but its effects were more potent and blissful than words can express. They had faded by degrees, yet they lingered long – and painted life in hues of splendour. Bertha often wondered at my lightness of heart and unaccustomed gaiety; for, before, I had been rather serious, or even sad, in my disposition. She loved me the better for my cheerful temper, and our days were winged by joy.

Five years afterwards I was suddenly summoned to the bedside of the dying Cornelius. He had sent for me in haste, conjuring my instant presence. I found him stretched on his pallet, enfeebled even to death; all of life that yet remained animated his piercing eyes, and they were fixed on a glass vessel, full of a roseate liquid.

"Behold," he said, in a broken and inward voice, "the vanity of human wishes! a second time my hopes are about to be crowned, a second time they are destroyed. Look at that liquor – you remember five years ago I had prepared the same, with the same success; – then, as now, my thirsting lips expected to taste the immortal elixir – you dashed it from me! and at present it is too late."

He spoke with difficulty, and fell back on his pillow. I could not help saying,—

"How, revered master, can a cure for love restore you to life?"

A faint smile gleamed across his face as I listened earnestly to his scarcely intelligible answer.

"A cure for love and for all things – the Elixir of Immortality. Ah! if now I might drink, I should live for ever!"

As he spoke, a golden flash gleamed from the fluid; a well-remembered fragrance stole over the air; he raised himself, all weak as he was – strength seemed miraculously to re-enter his frame – he stretched forth his hand – a loud explosion startled me – a ray of fire shot up from the elixir, and the glass vessel which contained it was shivered to atoms! I turned my eyes towards the philosopher; he had fallen back – his eyes were glassy – his features rigid – he was dead!

But I lived, and was to live for ever! So said the unfortunate alchymist, and for a few days I believed his words. I remembered the glorious intoxication that had followed my stolen draught. I reflected on the change I had felt in my frame – in my soul. The bounding elasticity of the one – the buoyant lightness of the other. I surveyed myself in a mirror, and could perceive no change in my features during the space of the five years which had elapsed. I remembered the radiant hues and grateful scent of that delicious beverage – worthy the gift it was capable of bestowing – I was, then, IMMORTAL!

A few days after I laughed at my credulity. The old proverb, that "a prophet is least regarded in his own country," was true with respect to me and my defunct master. I loved him as a man – I respected him as a sage – but I derided the notion that he could command the powers of darkness, and laughed at the superstitious fears with which he was regarded by the vulgar. He was a wise philosopher, but had no acquaintance with any spirits but those clad in flesh and blood. His science was simply human; and human science, I soon persuaded myself, could never conquer nature's laws so far as to imprison the soul for ever within its carnal habitation. Cornelius had brewed a soul-refreshing drink – more inebriating than wine – sweeter and more fragrant than any fruit: it possessed probably strong medicinal powers, imparting gladness to the heart and vigour to the limbs; but its effects would wear out; already were they diminished in my frame. I was a lucky fellow to have quaffed health and joyous spirits, and perhaps long life, at my master's hands; but my good fortune ended there: longevity was far different from immortality.

I continued to entertain this belief for many years. Sometimes a thought stole across me – Was the alchymist indeed deceived? But my habitual credence was, that I should meet the fate of all the children of Adam at my appointed time – a little late, but still at a natural age. Yet it was certain that I retained a wonderfully youthful look. I was laughed at for my vanity in consulting the mirror so often, but I consulted it in vain – my brow was untrenched – my cheeks – my eyes – my whole person continued as untarnished as in my twentieth year.

I was troubled. I looked at the faded beauty of Bertha – I seemed more like her son. By degrees our neighbours began to make similar observations, and I found at last that I went by the name of the Scholar bewitched. Bertha herself grew uneasy. She became jealous and peevish, and at length she began to question me. We had no children; we were all in all to each other; and though, as she grew older, her vivacious spirit became a little allied to ill-temper, and her beauty sadly diminished, I cherished her in my heart as the mistress I had idolized, the wife I had sought and won with such perfect love.

At last our situation became intolerable: Bertha was fifty – I twenty years of age. I had, in very shame, in some measure adopted the habits of a more advanced age; I no longer mingled in the dance among the young and gay, but my heart bounded along with them while I restrained my feet; and a sorry figure I cut among the Nestors of our village. But before the time I mention, things were altered – we were universally shunned; we were – at least, I was – reported to have kept up an iniquitous acquaintance with some of my former master's supposed friends. Poor Bertha was pitied, but deserted. I was regarded with horror and detestation.

What was to be done? we sat by our winter fire – poverty had made itself felt, for none would buy the produce of my farm; and often I had been forced to journey twenty miles, to some place where I was not known, to dispose of our property. It is true, we had saved something for an evil day – that day was come.

We sat by our lone fireside – the old-hearted youth and his antiquated wife. Again Bertha insisted on knowing the truth; she recapitulated all she had ever heard said about me, and added her own observations. She conjured me to cast off the spell; she described how much more comely grey hairs were than my chestnut locks; she descanted on the reverence and respect due to age – how preferable to the slight regard paid to mere children: could I imagine that the despicable gifts of youth and good looks outweighed disgrace, hatred, and scorn? Nay, in the end I should be burnt as a dealer in the black art, while she, to whom I had not deigned to communicate any portion of my good fortune, might be stoned as my accomplice. At length she insinuated that I must share my secret with her, and bestow on her like benefits to those I myself enjoyed, or she would denounce me – and then she burst into tears.

Thus beset, methought it was the best way to tell the truth. I revealed it as tenderly as I could, and spoke only of a *very long life*, not of immortality – which representation, indeed, coincided best with my own ideas. When I ended, I rose and said,—

"And now, my Bertha, will you denounce the lover of your youth? – You will not, I know. But it is too hard, my poor wife, that you should suffer from my ill-luck and the accursed arts of Cornelius. I will leave you – you have wealth enough, and friends will return in my absence. I will go; young as I seem, and strong as I am, I can work and gain my bread among strangers, unsuspected and unknown. I loved you in youth;

God is my witness that I would not desert you in age, but that your safety and happiness require it."

I took my cap and moved towards the door; in a moment Bertha's arms were round my neck, and her lips were pressed to mine. "No, my husband, my Winzy," she said, "you shall not go alone – take me with you; we will remove from this place, and, as you say, among strangers we shall be unsuspected and safe. I am not so very old as quite to shame you, my Winzy; and I daresay the charm will soon wear off, and, with the blessing of God, you will become more elderly-looking, as is fitting; you shall not leave me."

I returned the good soul's embrace heartily. "I will not, my Bertha; but for your sake I had not thought of such a thing. I will be your true, faithful husband while you are spared to me, and do my duty by you to the last."

The next day we prepared secretly for our emigration. We were obliged to make great pecuniary sacrifices – it could not be helped. We realized a sum sufficient, at least, to maintain us while Bertha lived; and, without saying adieu to any one, quitted our native country to take refuge in a remote part of western France.

It was a cruel thing to transport poor Bertha from her native village, and the friends of her youth, to a new country, new language, new customs. The strange secret of my destiny rendered this removal immaterial to me; but I compassionated her deeply, and was glad to perceive that she found compensation for her misfortunes in a variety of little ridiculous circumstances. Away from all tell-tale chroniclers, she sought to decrease the apparent disparity of our ages by a thousand feminine arts – rouge, youthful dress, and assumed juvenility of manner. I could not be angry. Did not I myself wear a mask? Why quarrel with hers, because it was less successful? I grieved deeply when I remembered that this was my Bertha, whom I had loved so fondly, and won with such transport – the dark-eyed, dark-haired girl, with smiles of enchanting archness and a step like a fawn – this mincing, simpering, jealous old woman. I should have revered her grey locks and withered cheeks; but thus! – It was my work, I knew; but I did not the less deplore this type of human weakness.

Her jealousy never slept. Her chief occupation was to discover that, in spite of outward appearances, I was myself growing old. I verily believe that the poor soul loved me truly in her heart, but never had woman so tormenting a mode of displaying fondness. She would discern wrinkles in my face and decrepitude in my walk, while I bounded along in youthful vigour, the youngest looking of twenty youths. I never dared address another woman. On one occasion, fancying that the belle of the village regarded me with favouring eyes, she brought me a grey wig. Her constant discourse among her acquaintances was, that though I looked so young, there was ruin at work within my frame; and she affirmed that the worst symptom about me was my apparent health. My youth was a disease, she said, and I ought at all times to prepare, if not for a sudden and awful death, at least to awake some morning white-headed and bowed down with all the marks of advanced years. I let her talk – I often joined in her conjectures. Her warnings chimed in with my never-ceasing speculations concerning my state, and I took an earnest, though painful, interest in listening to all that her quick wit and excited imagination could say on the subject.

Why dwell on these minute circumstances? We lived on for many long years. Bertha became bedrid and paralytic; I nursed her as a mother might a child. She grew peevish, and still harped upon one string – of how long I should survive her. It has ever been a source of consolation to me, that I performed my duty scrupulously towards her. She had been mine in youth, she was mine in age; and at last, when I heaped the sod over her corpse, I wept to feel that I had lost all that really bound me to humanity.

Since then how many have been my cares and woes, how few and empty my enjoyments! I pause here in my history – I will pursue it no further. A sailor without rudder or compass, tossed on a stormy sea – a traveller lost on a widespread heath, without landmark or stone to guide him – such have I been: more lost, more hopeless than either. A nearing ship, a gleam from some far cot, may save them; but I have no beacon except the hope of death.

Death! mysterious, ill-visaged friend of weak humanity! Why alone of all mortals have you cast me from your sheltering fold? Oh, for the peace of the grave! the deep silence of the iron-bound tomb! that thought would cease to work in my brain, and my heart beat no more with emotions varied only by new forms of sadness!

Am I immortal? I return to my first question. In the first place, is it not more probable that the beverage of the alchymist was fraught rather with longevity than eternal life? Such is my hope. And then be it remembered, that I only drank *half* of the potion prepared by him. Was not the whole necessary to complete the charm? To have drained half the Elixir of Immortality is but to be half-immortal – my For-ever is thus truncated and null.

But again, who shall number the years of the half of eternity? I often try to imagine by what rule the infinite may be divided. Sometimes I fancy age advancing upon me. One grey hair I have found. Fool! do I lament? Yes, the fear of age and death often creeps coldly into my heart; and the more I live, the more I dread death, even while I abhor life. Such an enigma is man – born to perish – when he wars, as I do, against the established laws of his nature.

But for this anomaly of feeling surely I might die: the medicine of the alchymist would not be proof against fire – sword – and the strangling waters. I have gazed upon the blue depths of many a placid lake, and the tumultuous rushing of many a mighty river, and have said, peace inhabits those waters; yet I have turned my steps away, to live yet another day. I have asked myself, whether suicide would be a crime in one to whom thus only the portals of the other world could be opened. I have done all, except presenting myself as a soldier or duellist, an object of destruction to my – no, *not* my fellow-mortals, and therefore I have shrunk away. They are not my fellows. The inextinguishable power of life in my frame, and their ephemeral existence, places us wide as the poles asunder. I could not raise a hand against the meanest or the most powerful among them.

Thus I have lived on for many a year – alone, and weary of myself – desirous of death, yet never dying – a mortal immortal. Neither ambition nor avarice can enter my mind, and the ardent love that gnaws at my heart, never to be returned – never to find an equal on which to expend itself – lives there only to torment me.

This very day I conceived a design by which I may end all – without self-slaughter, without making another man a Cain – an expedition, which mortal frame can never survive, even endued with the youth and strength that inhabits mine. Thus I shall put my immortality to the test, and rest for ever – or return, the wonder and benefactor of the human species.

Before I go, a miserable vanity has caused me to pen these pages. I would not die, and leave no name behind. Three centuries have passed since I quaffed the fatal beverage; another year shall not elapse before, encountering gigantic dangers – warring with the powers of frost in their home – beset by famine, toil, and tempest – I yield this body, too tenacious a cage for a soul which thirsts for freedom, to the destructive elements of air and water; or, if I survive, my name shall be recorded as one of the most famous among the sons of men; and, my task achieved, I shall adopt more resolute means, and, by scattering and annihilating the atoms that compose my frame, set at liberty the life imprisoned within, and so cruelly prevented from soaring from this dim earth to a sphere more congenial to its immortal essence.

THE INVISIBLE GIRL

This slender narrative has no pretensions to the regularity of a story, or the development of situations and feelings; it is but a slight sketch, delivered nearly as it was narrated to me by one of the humblest of the actors concerned: nor will I spin out a circumstance interesting principally from its singularity and truth, but narrate, as concisely as I can, how I was surprised on visiting what seemed a ruined tower, crowning a bleak promontory overhanging the sea, that flows between Wales and Ireland, to find that though the exterior preserved all the savage rudeness that betokened many a war with the elements, the interior was fitted up somewhat in the guise of a sum-mer-house, for it was too small to deserve any other name. It consisted but of the ground-floor, which served as an entrance, and one room above, which was reached by a staircase made out of the thickness of the wall. This chamber was floored and carpeted, decorated with elegant furniture; and, above all, to attract the attention and excite curiosity, there hung over the chimney-piece – for to preserve the apartment from damp a fireplace had been built evidently since it had assumed a guise so dissimilar to the object of its construction – a picture simply painted in water-colours, which deemed more than any part of the adornments of the room to be at war with the rudeness of the building, the solitude in which it was placed, and the des-olation of the surrounding scenery. This drawing represented a lovely girl in the very pride and bloom of youth; her dress was simple, in the fashion of the beginning of the eighteenth century; her countenance was embellished by a look of mingled innocence and intelligence, to which was added the imprint of serenity of soul and natural cheerfulness. She was reading one of those folio romances which have so long been the delight of the enthusiastic and young; her mandoline was at her feet – her parroquet perched on a huge mirror near her; the arrangement of furniture and hangings gave token of a luxurious dwelling, and her attire also evidently that of home and privacy, yet bore with it an appearance of ease and girlish ornament, as if she wished to please. Beneath this picture was inscribed in golden letters, "The Invisible Girl."

Rambling about a country nearly uninhabited, having lost my way, and being overtaken by a shower, I had lighted on this dreary-looking tenement, which seemed to rock in the blast, and to be hung up there as the very symbol of desolation. I was gazing wistfully and cursing inwardly my stars which led me to a ruin that could afford no shelter, though the storm began to pelt more seriously than before, when I saw an old woman's head popped out from a kind of loophole, and as suddenly withdrawn; – a minute after a feminine voice called to me from within, and penetrating a little brambly maze that screened a door, which I had not before observed, so skilfully had the planter succeeded in concealing art with nature, I found the good dame standing on the threshold and inviting me to take refuge within. "I had just come up from our cot hard by," she said, "to look after the things, as I do every day, when the rain came on – will ye walk up till it is over?" I was about to observe that the cot hard by, at the venture of a few rain drops, was better than a ruined tower, and to ask my kind hostess whether "the things" were pigeons or crows that she was come to look after, when the matting of the floor and the carpeting of the staircase struck my eye. I was still more surprised when I saw the room above; and beyond all, the picture and its singular inscription, naming her invisible, whom the painter had coloured forth into very agreeable visibility, awakened my most lively curiosity; the result of this, of my exceeding politeness towards the old woman, and her own natural garrulity, was a kind of garbled narrative which my imagination eked out, and future inquiries rectified, till it assumed the following form.

Some years before, in the afternoon of a September day, which, though tolerably fair, gave many tokens of a tempestuous night, a gentleman arrived at a little coast town about ten miles from this place; he expressed his desire to hire a boat to carry him to the town of – about fifteen miles farther on the coast. The menaces which the sky held forth made the fishermen loathe to venture, till at length two, one the father of a numerous family, bribed by the bountiful reward the stranger promised, the other, the son of my hostess, induced by youthful daring, agreed to undertake the voyage. The wind was fair, and they hoped to make good way before nightfall, and to get into port ere the rising of the storm. They pushed off with good cheer, at least the fishermen did; as for the stranger, the deep mourning which he wore was not half so black as the melancholy that wrapt his mind. He looked as if he had never smiled – as if some unutterable thought, dark as night and bitter as death, had built its nest within his bosom, and brooded therein eternally; he did not mention his name; but one of the villagers recognised him as Henry Vernon, the son of a baronet who possessed a mansion about three miles distant from the town for which he was bound. This mansion was almost abandoned by the family; but Henry had, in a romantic fit, visited it about three years before, and Sir Peter had been down there during the previous spring for about a couple of months.

The boat did not make so much way as was expected; the breeze failed them as they got out to sea, and they were fain with oar as well as sail to try to weather the promontory that jutted out between them and the spot they desired to reach. They were yet far distant when the shifting wind began to exert its strength, and to blow with violent though unequal blasts.

Night came on pitchy dark, and the howling waves rose and broke with frightful violence, menacing to overwhelm the tiny bark that dared resist their fury. They were forced to lower every sail, and take to their oars; one man was obliged to bale out the water, and Vernon himself took an oar, and rowing with desperate energy, equalled the force of the more practised boatmen. There had been much talk between the sailors before the tempest came on; now, except a brief command, all were silent. One thought of his wife and children, and silently cursed the caprice of the stranger that endangered in its effects, not only his life, but their welfare; the other feared less, for he was a daring lad, but he worked hard, and had no time for speech; while Vernon bitterly regretting the thoughtlessness which had made him cause others to share a peril, unimportant as far as he himself was concerned, now tried to cheer them with a voice full of animation and courage, and now pulled yet more strongly at the oar he held. The only person who did not seem wholly intent on the work he was about, was the man who baled; every now and then he gazed intently round, as if the sea held afar off, on its tumultuous waste, some object that he strained his eyes to discern. But all was blank, except as the crests of the high waves showed themselves, or far out on the verge of the horizon, a kind of lifting of the clouds betokened greater violence for the blast. At length he exclaimed, "Yes, I see it! – the larboard oar! – now! if we can make yonder light, we are saved!" Both the rowers instinctively turned their heads, – but cheerless darkness answered their gaze.

"You cannot see it," cried their companion, "but we are nearing it; and, please God, we shall outlive this night." Soon he took the oar from Vernon's hand, who, quite exhausted, was failing in his strokes. He rose and looked for the beacon which promised them safety; – it glimmered with so faint a ray, that now he said, "I see it;" and again, "it is nothing:" still, as they made way, it dawned upon his sight, growing more steady and distinct as it beamed across the lurid waters, which themselves became smoother, so that safety seemed to arise from the bosom of the ocean under the influence of that flickering gleam.

"What beacon is it that helps us at our need?" asked Vernon, as the men, now able to manage their oars with greater ease, found breath to answer his question.

"A fairy one, I believe," replied the elder sailor, "yet no less a true: it burns in an old tumble-down tower, built on the top of a rock which looks over the sea. We never saw it before this summer; and now each night it is to be seen, – at least when it is looked for, for we cannot see it from our village; – and it is such an out-of-the-way place that no one has need to go near it, except through a chance like this. Some say it is burnt by witches, some say by smugglers; but this I know, two parties have been to search, and found nothing but the bare walls of the tower. All is deserted by day, and dark by night; for no light was to be seen while we were there, though it burned sprightly enough when we were out at sea."

"I have heard say," observed the younger sailor, "it is burnt by the ghost of a maiden who lost her sweetheart in these parts; he being wrecked, and his body found at the foot of the tower: she goes by the name among us of the 'Invisible Girl.'"

The voyagers had now reached the landing-place at the foot of the tower. Vernon cast a glance upward, – the light was still burning. With some difficulty, struggling with the breakers, and blinded by night, they contrived to get their little bark to shore, and to draw her up on the beach. They then scrambled up the precipitous pathway, overgrown by weeds and underwood, and, guided by the more experienced fisherman, they found the entrance to the tower; door or gate there was none, and all was dark as the tomb, and silent and almost as cold as death.

"This will never do," said Vernon; "surely our hostess will show her light, if not herself, and guide our darkling steps by some sign of life and comfort."

"We will get to the upper chamber," said the sailor, "if I can but hit upon the broken-down steps; but you will find no trace of the Invisible Girl nor her light either, I warrant."

"Truly a romantic adventure of the most disagreeable kind," muttered Vernon, as he stumbled over the unequal ground; "she of the beacon-light must be both ugly and old, or she would not be so peevish and inhospitable."

With considerable difficulty, and after divers knocks and bruises, the adventurers at length succeeded in reaching the upper storey; but all was blank and bare, and they were fain to stretch themselves on the hard floor, when weariness, both of mind and body, conduced to steep their senses in sleep.

Long and sound were the slumbers of the mariners. Vernon but forgot himself for an hour; then throwing off drowsiness, and finding his rough couch uncongenial to repose, he got up and placed himself at the hole that served for a window – for glass there was none, and there being not even a rough bench, he leant his back against the embrasure, as the only rest he could find. He had forgotten his danger, the mysterious beacon, and its invisible guardian: his thoughts were occupied on the horrors of his own fate, and the unspeakable wretchedness that sat like a nightmare on his heart.

It would require a good-sized volume to relate the causes which had changed the once happy Vernon into the most woful mourner that ever clung to the outer trappings of grief, as slight though cherished symbols of the wretchedness within. Henry was the only child of Sir Peter Vernon, and as much spoiled by his father's idolatry as the old baronet's violent and tyrannical temper would permit. A young orphan was educated in his father's house, who in the same way was treated with generosity and kindness, and yet who lived in deep awe of Sir Peter's authority, who was a widower; and these two children were all he had to exert his power over, or to whom to extend his affection. Rosina was a cheerful-tempered girl, a little timid, and careful to avoid displeasing her protector; but so docile, so kind-hearted, and so affectionate, that she felt even less than Henry the discordant spirit of his parent. It is a tale often told; they were playmates and companions in childhood, and lovers in after days. Rosina was frightened to imagine that this secret affection, and the vows they pledged, might be disapproved of by Sir Peter. But sometimes she consoled herself by thinking that perhaps she was in reality her Henry's destined bride, brought up with him under the design of their future union; and Henry, while he felt that this was not the case, resolved to wait only until he was of age to declare and accomplish his wishes in making the sweet Rosina his wife. Meanwhile he was careful to avoid premature discovery of his intentions, so to secure his beloved girl from persecution and insult. The old gentleman was very conveniently blind; he lived always in the country, and the lovers spent their lives together, unrebuked and uncontrolled. It was enough that Rosina played on her mandoline, and sang Sir Peter to sleep every day after dinner; she was the sole female in the house above the rank of a servant, and had her own way in the disposal of her time. Even when Sir Peter frowned, her innocent caresses and sweet voice were powerful to smooth the rough current of his temper. If ever human spirit lived in an earthly paradise, Rosina did at this time: her pure love was made happy by Henry's constant presence; and the confidence they felt in each other, and the security with which they looked forward to the future, rendered their path one of roses under a cloudless sky. Sir Peter was the slight drawback that only rendered their *tête-à-tête* more delightful, and gave value to the sympathy they each bestowed on the other. All at once an ominous personage made its appearance in Vernon Place, in the shape of a widow sister of Sir Peter, who, having succeeded in killing her husband and children with the effects of her vile temper, came, like a harpy, greedy for new prey, under her brother's roof. She too soon detected the attachment of the unsuspicious pair. She made all speed to impart her discovery to her brother, and at once to restrain and inflame his rage. Through her contrivance Henry was suddenly despatched on his travels abroad, that the coast might be clear for the persecution of Rosina; and then the richest of the lovely girl's many admirers, whom, under Sir Peter's single reign, she was allowed, nay, almost commanded, to dismiss, so desirous was he of keeping her for his own comfort, was selected, and she was ordered to marry him. The scenes of violence to which she was now exposed, the bitter taunts of the odious Mrs. Bainbridge, and the reckless fury of Sir Peter, were the more frightful and overwhelming from their novelty. To all she could only oppose a silent, tearful, but immutable steadiness of purpose: no threats, no rage could extort from her more than a touching prayer that they would not hate her, because she could not obey.

"There must be something we don't see under all this," said Mrs. Bainbridge; "take my word for it, brother, she corresponds secretly with Henry. Let us take her down to your seat in Wales, where she will have no pensioned beggars to assist her; and we shall see if her spirit be not bent to our purpose."

Sir Peter consented, and they all three took up their abode in the solitary and dreary-looking house before alluded to as belonging to the family. Here poor Rosina's sufferings grew intolerable. Before, surrounded by well-known scenes, and in perpetual intercourse with kind and familiar faces, she had not despaired in the end of conquering by her patience the cruelty of her persecutors; – nor had she written to Henry, for his name had not been mentioned by his relatives, nor their attachment alluded to, and she felt an instinctive wish to escape the dangers about her without his being annoyed, or the sacred secret of her love being laid bare, and wronged by the vulgar abuse of his aunt or the bitter curses of his father. But when she was taken to Wales, and made a prisoner in her apartment, when the flinty mountains about her seemed feebly to imitate the stony hearts she had to deal with, her courage began to fail. The only attendant permitted to approach her was Mrs. Bainbridge's maid; and under the tutelage of her fiend-like mistress, this woman was used as a decoy to entice the poor prisoner into confidence, and then to be betrayed. The simple, kind-hearted Rosina was a facile dupe, and at last, in the excess of her despair, wrote to Henry, and gave the letter to this woman to be forwarded. The letter in itself would have softened marble; it did not speak of their mutual vows, it but asked him to intercede with his father, that he would restore her to the place she had formerly held in his affections, and cease from a cruelty that would destroy her. "For I may die," wrote the hapless girl, "but marry another – never!" That single word, indeed, had sufficed to betray her secret, had it not been already discovered; as it was, it gave increased fury to Sir Peter, as his sister triumphantly pointed it out to him, for it need hardly be said that while the ink of the address was yet wet, and the seal still warm, Rosina's letter was carried to this lady. The culprit was summoned before them. What ensued none could tell; for their own sakes the cruel pair tried to palliate their part. Voices were high, and the soft murmur of Rosina's tone was lost in the howling of Sir Peter and the snarling of his sister. "Out of doors you shall go," roared the old man; "under my roof you shall not spend another night." And the words infamous seductress, and worse, such as had never met the poor girl's ear before, were caught by listening servants; and to each angry speech of the baronet, Mrs. Bainbridge added an envenomed point worse than all.

More dead then alive, Rosina was at last dismissed. Whether guided by despair, whether she took Sir Peter's threats literally, or whether his sister's orders were more decisive, none knew, but Rosina left the house; a servant saw her cross the park, weeping, and wringing her hands as she went. What became of her none could tell; her disappearance was not disclosed to Sir Peter till the following day, and then he showed by his anxiety to trace her steps and to find her, that his words had been but idle threats. The truth was, that though Sir Peter went to frightful lengths to prevent the marriage of the heir of his house with the portionless orphan, the object of his charity, yet in his heart he loved Rosina, and half his violence to her rose from anger at himself for treating her so ill. Now remorse began to sting him, as messenger after messenger came back without tidings of his victim. He dared not confess his worst fears to himself; and when his inhuman sister, trying to harden her conscience by angry words, cried, "The vile hussy has too surely made away with herself out of revenge to us," an oath the most tremendous, and a look sufficient to make even her tremble, commanded her silence. Her conjecture, however, appeared too true: a dark and rushing stream that flowed at the extremity of the park had doubtless received the lovely form, and quenched the life of this unfortunate girl. Sir Peter, when his endeavours to find her proved fruitless, returned to town, haunted by the image of his victim, and forced to acknowledge in his own heart that he would willingly lay down his life, could he see her again, even though it were as the bride of his son – his son, before whose questioning he quailed like the veriest coward; for when Henry was told of the death of Rosina, he suddenly returned from abroad to ask the cause – to visit her grave, and mourn her loss in the groves and valleys which had been the scenes of their mutual happiness. He made a thousand inquiries, and an ominous silence alone replied. Growing more earnest and more anxious, at length he drew from servants and dependents, and his odious aunt herself, the whole dreadful truth. From that moment despair struck his heart, and misery named him her own. He fled from his father's presence; and the recollection that one whom he ought to revere was guilty of so dark a crime, haunted him, as of old the Eumenides tormented the souls of men given up to their torturings. His first, his only wish, was to visit Wales, and to learn if any new discovery had been made, and whether it were possible to recover the mortal remains of the lost Rosina, so to satisfy the unquiet longings of his miserable heart. On this expedition was he bound when he made his appearance at the village before named; and now, in the deserted tower, his thoughts were busy with images of despair and death, and what his beloved one had suffered before her gentle nature had been goaded to such a deed of woe.

While immersed in gloomy reverie, to which the monotonous roaring of the sea made fit accompaniment, hours flew on, and Vernon was at last aware that the light of morning was creeping from out its eastern retreat, and dawning over the wild ocean, which still broke in furious tumult on the rocky beach. His companions now roused themselves, and prepared to depart. The food they had brought with them was damaged by sea-water, and their hunger, after hard labour and many hours' fasting, had become ravenous. It was impossible to put to sea in their shattered boat; but there stood a fisher's cot about two miles off, in a recess in the bay, of which the promontory on which the tower stood formed one side; and to this they hastened to repair. They did not spend a second thought on the light which had saved them, nor its cause, but left the ruin in search of a more hospitable asylum. Vernon cast his eyes round as he quitted it, but no vestige of an inhabitant met his eye, and he began to persuade himself that the beacon had been a creation of fancy merely. Arriving at the cottage in question, which was inhabited by a fisherman and his family, they made a homely breakfast, and then prepared to return to the tower, to refit their boat, and, if possible, bring her round. Vernon accompanied them, together with their host and his son. Several questions were asked concerning the Invisible Girl and her light, each agreeing that the apparition was novel, and not one being able to give even an explanation of how the name had become affixed to the unknown cause of this singular appearance; though both of the men of the cottage affirmed that once or twice they had seen a female figure in the adjacent wood, and that now and then a stranger girl made her appearance at another cot a mile off, on the other side of the promontory, and bought bread; they suspected both these to be the same, but could not tell. The inhabitants of the cot, indeed, appeared too stupid even to feel curiosity, and had never made any attempt at discovery. The whole day was spent by the sailors in repairing the boat; and the sound of hammers, and the voices of the men at work, resounded along the coast, mingled with the dashing of the waves. This was no time to explore the ruin for one who, whether human or supernatural, so evidently withdrew herself from intercourse with every living being.

Vernon, however, went over the tower, and searched every nook in vain. The dingy bare walls bore no token of serving as a shelter; and even a little recess in the wall of the staircase, which he had not before observed, was equally empty and desolate. Quitting the tower, he wandered in the pine wood that surrounded it, and, giving up all thought of solving the mystery, was soon engrossed by thoughts that touched his heart more nearly, when suddenly there appeared on the ground at his feet the vision of a slipper. Since Cinderella so tiny a slipper had never been seen; as plain as shoe could speak, it told a tale of elegance, loveliness, and youth. Vernon picked it up. He had often admired Rosina's singularly small foot, and his first thought was a question whether this little slipper would have fitted it. It was very strange! – it must belong to the Invisible Girl. Then there was a fairy form that kindled that light – a form of such material substance that its foot needed to be shod; and yet how shod? – with kid so fine, and of shape so exquisite, that it exactly resembled such as Rosina wore! Again the recurrence of the image of the beloved dead came forcibly across him; and a thousand home-felt associations, childish yet sweet, and lover-like though trifling, so filled Vernon's heart, that he threw himself his length on the ground, and wept more bitterly than ever the miserable fate of the sweet orphan.

In the evening the men quitted their work, and Vernon returned with them to the cot where they were to sleep, intending to pursue their voyage, weather permitting, the following morning. Vernon said nothing of his slipper, but returned with his rough associates. Often he looked back; but the tower rose darkly over the dim waves, and no light appeared. Preparations had been made in the cot for their accommodation, and the only bed in it was offered Vernon; but he refused to deprive his hostess, and, spreading his cloak on a heap of dry leaves, endeavoured to give himself up to repose. He slept for some hours; and when he awoke, all was still, save that the hard breathing of the sleepers in the same room with him interrupted the silence. He rose, and, going to the window, looked out over the now placid sea towards the mystic tower. The light was burning there, sending its slender rays across the waves. Congratulating himself on a circumstance he had not anticipated, Vernon softly left the cottage, and, wrapping his cloak round him, walked with a swift pace round the bay towards the tower. He reached it; still the light was burning. To enter and restore the maiden her shoe, would be but an act of courtesy; and Vernon intended to do this with such caution as to come unaware, before its wearer could, with her accustomed arts, withdraw herself from his eyes; but, unluckily, while yet making his way up the narrow pathway, his foot dislodged a loose fragment, that fell with crash and sound down the precipice. He sprung forward, on this, to retrieve by speed the advantage he had lost by this unlucky accident. He reached the door; he entered: all was silent, but also all was dark. He paused in the room below; he felt sure that a slight sound met his ear. He ascended the steps, and entered the upper chamber; but blank obscurity met his penetrating gaze, the starless night admitted not even a twilight glimmer through the only aperture. He closed his eyes, to try, on opening them again, to be able to catch some faint, wandering ray on the visual nerve; but it was in vain. He groped round the room; he stood still, and held his breath; and then, listening intently, he felt sure that another occupied the chamber with him, and that its atmosphere was slightly agitated by another's respiration. He remembered the recess in the staircase; but before he approached it he spoke; – he hesitated a moment what to say. "I must believe," he said, "that misfortune alone can cause your seclusion; and if the assistance of a man – of a gentleman"—

An exclamation interrupted him; a voice from the grave spoke his name – the accents of Rosina syllabled, "Henry! – is it indeed Henry whom I hear?"

He rushed forward, directed by the sound, and clasped in his arms the living form of his own lamented girl – his own Invisible Girl he called her; for even yet, as he felt her heart beat near his, and as he entwined her waist with his arm, supporting her as she almost sank to the ground with agitation, he could not see her; and, as her sobs prevented her speech, no sense but the instinctive one that filled his heart with tumultuous gladness, told him that the slender, wasted form he pressed so fondly was the living shadow of the Hebe beauty he had adored.

The morning saw this pair thus strangely restored to each other on the tranquil sea, sailing with a fair wind for L − , whence they were to proceed to Sir Peter's seat, which, three months before, Rosina had quitted in such agony and terror. The morning light dispelled the shadows that had veiled her, and disclosed the fair person of the Invisible Girl. Altered indeed she was by suffering and woe, but still the same sweet smile played on her lips, and the tender light of her soft blue eyes were all her own. Vernon drew out the slipper, and showed the cause that had occasioned him to resolve to discover the guardian of the mystic beacon; even now he dared not inquire how she had existed in that desolate spot, or wherefore she had so sedulously avoided observation, when the right thing to have been done was to have sought him immediately, under whose care, protected by whose love, no danger need be feared. But Rosina shrunk from him as he spoke, and a deathlike pallor came over her cheek, as she faintly whispered, "Your father's curse – your father's dreadful threats!" It appeared, indeed, that Sir Peter's violence, and the cruelty of Mrs. Bainbridge, had succeeded in impressing Rosina with wild and unvanquishable terror. She had fled from their house without plan or forethought – driven by frantic horror and overwhelming fear, she had left it with scarcely any money, and there seemed to her no possibility of either returning or proceeding onward. She had no friend except Henry in the wide world; whither could she go? – to have sought Henry would have sealed their fates to misery; for, with an oath, Sir Peter had declared he would rather see them both in their coffins than married. After wandering about, hiding by day, and only venturing forth at night, she had come to this deserted tower, which seemed a place of refuge. How she had lived since then she could hardly tell: she had lingered in the woods by day, or slept in the vault of the tower, an asylum none were acquainted with or had discovered: by night she burned the pinecones of the wood, and night was her dearest time; for it seemed to her as if security came with darkness. She was unaware that Sir Peter had left that part of the country, and was terrified lest her hiding-place should be revealed to him. Her only hope was that Henry would return – that Henry would never rest till he had found her. She confessed that the long interval and the approach of winter had visited her with dismay; she feared that, as her strength was failing, and her form wasting to a skeleton, that she might die, and never see her own Henry more.

An illness, indeed, in spite of all his care, followed her restoration to security and the comforts of civilised life; many months went by before the bloom revisiting her cheeks, and her limbs regaining their roundness, she resembled once more the picture drawn of her in her days of bliss before any visitation of sorrow. It was a copy of this portrait that decorated the tower, the scene of her suffering, in which I had found shelter. Sir Peter, overjoyed to be relieved from the pangs of remorse, and delighted again to see his orphan ward, whom he really loved, was now as eager as before he had been averse to bless her union with his son. Mrs. Bainbridge they never saw again. But each year they spent a few months in their Welsh mansion, the scene of their early wedded happiness, and the spot where again poor Rosina had awoke to life and joy after her cruel persecutions. Henry's fond care had fitted up the tower, and decorated it as I saw; and often did he come over, with his "Invisible Girl," to renew, in the very scene of its occurrence, the remembrance of all the incidents which had led to their meeting again, during the shades of night, in that sequestered ruin.

97

THE SISTERS OF ALBANO

"And near Albano's scarce divided waves
Shine from a sister valley; – and afar
The Tiber winds, and the broad ocean laves
The Latian coast where sprang the Epic war,
'Arms and the Man,' whose re-ascending star
Rose o'er an empire; but beneath thy right
Tully reposed from Rome; and where yon bar
Of girdling mountains intercepts the sight
The Sabine farm was till'd, the weary bard's delight."

It was to see this beautiful lake that I made my last excursion before quitting Rome. The spring had nearly grown into summer, the trees were all in full but fresh green foliage, the vine-dresser was singing, perched among them, training his vines: the cicada had not yet begun her song, the heats therefore had not commenced; but at evening the fire-flies gleamed among the hills, and the cooing aziola assured us of what in that country needs no assurance – fine weather for the morrow. We set out early in the morning to avoid the heats, breakfasted at Albano, and till ten o'clock passed our time in visiting the Mosaic, the villa of Cicero, and other curiosities of the place. We reposed during the middle of the day in a tent elevated for us at the hill-top, whence we looked on the hill-embosomed lake, and the distant eminence crowned by a town with its church. Other villages and cottages were scattered among the foldings of mountains, and beyond we saw the deep blue sea of the southern poets, which received the swift and immortal Tiber, rocking it to repose among its devouring waves. The Coliseum falls and the Pantheon decays, – the very hills of Rome are perishing, – but the Tiber lives for ever, flows for ever, and for ever feeds the land-encircled Mediterranean with fresh waters.

Our summer and pleasure-seeking party consisted of many: to me the most interesting person was the Countess Atanasia D – , who was as beautiful as an imagination of Raphael, and good as the ideal of a poet. Two of her children accompanied her, with animated looks and gentle manners, quiet, yet enjoying. I sat near her, watching the changing shadows of the landscape before us. As the sun descended, it poured a tide of light into the valley of the lake, deluging the deep bank formed by the mountain with liquid gold. The domes and turrets of the far town flashed and gleamed, the trees were dyed in splendour; two or three slight clouds, which had drunk the radiance till it became their essence, floated golden islets in the lustrous empyrean. The waters, reflecting the brilliancy of the sky and the fire-tinted banks, beamed a second heaven, a second irradiated earth, at our feet. The Mediterranean, gazing on the sun, – as the eyes of a mortal bride fail and are dimmed when reflecting her lover's glance, – was lost, mixed in his light, till it had become one with him. – Long (our souls, like the sea, the hills, and lake, drinking in the supreme loveliness) we gazed, till the too full cup overflowed, and we turned away with a sigh.

At our feet there was a knoll of ground, that formed the foreground of our picture; two trees lay basking against the sky, glittering with the golden light, which like dew seemed to hang amid their branches; a rock closed the prospect on the other side, twined round by creepers, and redolent with blooming myrtle; a brook, crossed by huge stones, gushed through the turf, and on the fragments of rock that lay about, sat two or three persons, peasants, who attracted our attention. One was a hunter, as his gun, lying on a bank not far off, demonstrated, yet he was a tiller of the soil; his rough straw hat, and his picturesque but coarse dress, belonged to that class. The other was some contadina, in the costume of her country, returning, her basket on her arm, from the village to her cottage home. They were regarding the stores of a pedlar, who with doffed hat stood near: some of these consisted of pictures and prints – views of the country, and portraits of the Madonna. Our peasants regarded these with pleased attention.

"One might easily make out a story for that pair," I said: "his gun is a help to the imagination, and we may fancy him a bandit with his contadina love, the terror of all the neighbourhood, except of her, the most defenceless being in it."

"You speak lightly of such a combination," said the lovely countess at my side, "as if it must not in its nature be the cause of dreadful tragedies. The mingling of love with crime is a dread conjunction, and lawless pursuits are never followed without bringing on the criminal, and all allied to him, ineffable misery. I speak with emotion, for your observation reminds me of an unfortunate girl, now one of the Sisters of Charity in the convent of Santa Chiara at Rome, whose unhappy passion for a man, such as you mention, spread destruction and sorrow widely around her."

I entreated my lovely friend to relate the history of the nun. For a long time she resisted my entreaties, as not willing to depress the spirit of a party of pleasure by a tale of sorrow. But I urged her, and she yielded. Her sweet Italian phraseology now rings in my ears, and her beautiful countenance is before me. As she spoke, the sun set, and the moon bent her silver horn in the ebbing tide of glory he had left. The lake changed from purple to silver, and the trees, before so splendid, now in dark masses, just reflected from their tops the mild moonlight. The fire-flies flashed among the rocks;

the bats circled round us: meanwhile thus commenced the Countess Atanasia:—

The nun of whom I speak had a sister older than herself; I can remember them when as children they brought eggs and fruit to my father's villa. Maria and Anina were constantly together. With their large straw hats to shield them from the scorching sun, they were at work in their father's *podere* all day, and in the evening, when Maria, who was the elder by four years, went to the fountain for water, Anina ran at her side. Their cot – the folding of the hill conceals it – is at the lake-side opposite; and about a quarter of a mile up the hill is the rustic fountain of which I speak. Maria was serious, gentle, and considerate; Anina was a laughing, merry little creature, with the face of a cherub. When Maria was fifteen, their mother fell ill, and was nursed at the convent of Santa Chiara at Rome. Maria attended her, never leaving her bedside day or night. The nuns thought her an angel, she deemed them saints: her mother died, and they persuaded her to make one of them; her father could not but acquiesce in her holy intention, and she became one of the Sisters of Charity, the nun-nurses of Santa Chiara. Once or twice a year she visited her home, gave sage and kind advice to Anina, and sometimes wept to part from her; but her piety and her active employments for the sick reconciled her to her fate. Anina was more sorry to lose her sister's society. The other girls of the village did not please her: she was a good child, and worked hard for her father, and her sweetest recompense was the report he made of her to Maria, and the fond praises and caresses the latter bestowed on her when they met.

It was not until she was fifteen that Anina showed any diminution of affection for her sister. Yet I cannot call it diminution, for she loved her perhaps more than ever, though her holy calling and sage lectures prevented her from reposing confidence, and made her tremble lest the nun, devoted to heaven and good works, should read in her eyes, and disapprove of the earthly passion that occupied her. Perhaps a part of her reluctance arose from the reports that were current against her lover's character, and certainly from the disapprobation and even hatred of him that her father frequently expressed. Ill-fated Anina! I know not if in the north your peasants love as ours; but the passion of Anina was entwined with the roots of her being, it was herself: she could die, but not cease to love. The dislike of her father for Domenico made their intercourse clandestine. He was always at the fountain to fill her pitcher, and lift it on her head. He attended the same mass; and when her father went to Albano, Velletri, or Rome, he seemed to learn by instinct the exact moment of his departure, and joined her in the *podere*, labouring with her and for her, till the old man was seen descending the mountain-path on his return. He said he worked for a contadino near Nemi. Anina sometimes wondered that he could spare so much time for her; but his excuses were plausible, and the result too delightful not to blind the innocent girl to its obvious cause.

Poor Domenico! the reports spread against him were too well founded: his sole excuse was that his father had been a robber before him, and he had spent his early years among these lawless men. He had better things in his nature, and yearned for the peace of the guiltless. Yet he could hardly be called guilty, for no dread crime stained him. Nevertheless, he was an outlaw and a bandit; and now that he loved Anina, these names were the stings of an adder to pierce his soul. He would have fled from his comrades to a far country, but Anina dwelt amid their very haunts. At this period also the police established by the French Government, which then possessed Rome, made these bands more alive to the conduct of their members; and rumours of active measures to be taken against those who occupied the hills near Albano, Nemi, and Velletri, caused them to draw together in tighter bonds. Domenico would not, if he could, desert his friends in the hour of danger.

On a *festa* at this time – it was towards the end of October – Anina strolled with her father among the villagers, who all over Italy make holiday by congregating and walking in one place. Their talk was entirely of the *ladri* and the French, and many terrible stories were related of the extirpation of banditti in the kingdom of Naples, and the mode by which the French succeeded in their undertaking was minutely described. The troops scoured the country, visiting one haunt of the robbers after the other, and dislodging them, tracked them as in those countries they hunt the wild beasts of the forest, till, drawing the circle narrower, they enclosed them in one spot. They then drew a cordon round the place, which they guarded with the utmost vigilance, forbidding any to enter it with provisions, on pain of instant death. And as this menace was rigorously executed, in a short time the besieged bandits were starved into a surrender. The French troops were now daily expected, for they had been seen at Velletri and Nemi; at the same time it was affirmed that several outlaws had taken up their abode at Rocca Giovane, a deserted village on the summit of one of these hills, and it was supposed that they would make that place the scene of their final retreat.

The next day, as Anina worked in the *podere*, a party of French horse passed by along the road that separated her garden from the lake. Curiosity made her look at them; and her beauty was too great not to attract. Their observations and address soon drove her away; for a woman in love consecrates herself to her lover, and deems the admiration of others to be profanation. She spoke to her father of the impertinence of these men; and he answered by rejoicing at their arrival, and the destruction of the lawless bands that would ensue. When in the evening Anina went to the fountain, she looked timidly around, and hoped that Domenico would be at his accustomed post, for the arrival of the French destroyed her feeling of security. She went rather later than usual, and a cloudy evening made it seem already dark; the wind roared among the trees, bending hither and thither even the stately cypresses; the waters of the lake were agitated into high waves, and dark masses of thundercloud lowered over the hill-tops, giving a lurid tinge to the landscape.

Anina passed quickly up the mountain-path. When she came in sight of the fountain, which was rudely hewn in the living rock, she saw Domenico leaning against a projection of the hill, his hat drawn over his eyes, his *tabaro* fallen from his shoulders, his arms folded in an attitude of dejection. He started when he saw her; his voice and phrases were broken and unconnected; yet he never gazed on her with such ardent love, nor solicited her to delay her departure with such impassioned tenderness.

"How glad I am to find you here!" she said; "I was fearful of meeting one of the French soldiers: I dread them even more than the banditti."

Domenico cast a look of eager inquiry on her, and then turned away, saying, "Sorry am I that I shall not be here to protect you. I am obliged to go to Rome for a week or two. You will be faithful, Anina mia; you will love me, though I never see you more?"

The interview, under these circumstances, was longer than usual. He led her down the path till they nearly came in sight of her cottage; still they lingered. A low whistle was heard among the myrtle underwood at the lake-side; he started; it was repeated; and he answered it by a similar note. Anina, terrified, was about to ask what this meant, when, for the first time, he pressed her to his heart, kissed her roseate lips, and, with a muttered "Carissima addio," left her, springing down the bank; and as she gazed in wonder, she thought she saw a boat cross a line of light made by the opening of a cloud. She stood long absorbed in reverie, wondering and remembering with thrilling pleasure the quick embrace and impassioned farewell of her lover. She delayed so long that her father came to seek her.

Each evening after this, Anina visited the fountain at the Ave Maria; he was not there: each day seemed an age; and incomprehensible fears occupied her heart. About a fortnight after, letters arrived from Maria. They came to say that she had been ill of the malaria fever, that she was now convalescent, but that change of air was necessary for her recovery, and that she had obtained leave to spend a month at home at Albano. She asked her father to come the next day to fetch her. These were pleasant tidings for Anina; she resolved to disclose everything to her sister, and during her long visit she doubted not but that she would contrive her happiness. Old Andrea departed the following morning, and the whole day was spent by the sweet girl in dreams of future bliss. In the evening Maria arrived, weak and wan, with all the marks of that dread illness about her, yet, as she assured her sister, feeling quite well.

As they sat at their frugal supper, several villagers came in to inquire for Maria; but all their talk was of the French soldiers and the robbers, of whom a band of at least twenty was collected in Rocca Giovane, strictly watched by the military.

"We may be grateful to the French," said Andrea, "for this good deed; the country will be rid of these ruffians."

"True, friend," said another; "but it is horrible to think what these men suffer: they have, it appears, exhausted all the food they brought with them to the village, and are literally starving. They have not an ounce of maccaroni among them; and a poor fellow who was taken and executed yesterday was a mere anatomy: you could tell every bone in his skin."

"There was a sad story the other day," said another, "of an old man from Nemi, whose son, they say, is among them at Rocca Giovane: he was found within the lines with some *baccallà* under his *pastrano*, and shot on the spot."

"There is not a more desperate gang," observed the first speaker, "in the states and the *regno* put together. They have sworn never to yield but upon good terms. To secure these, their plan is to waylay passengers and make prisoners, whom they keep as hostages for mild treatment from the Government. But the French are merciless; they are better pleased that the bandits wreak their vengeance on these poor creatures than spare one of their lives."

"They have captured two persons already," said another;

"and there is old Betta Tossi half frantic, for she is sure her son is taken: he has not been at home these ten days."

"I should rather guess," said an old man, "that he went there with good-will: the young scapegrace kept company with Domenico Baldi of Nemi."

"No worse company could he have kept in the whole country," said Andrea; "Domenico is the bad son of a bad race. Is he in the village with the rest?"

"My own eyes assured me of that," replied the other.

"When I was up the hill with eggs and fowls to the piquette there, I saw the branches of an ilex move; the poor fellow was weak perhaps, and could not keep his hold; presently he dropped to the ground; every musket was levelled at him, but he started up and was away like a hare among the rocks. Once he turned, and then I saw Domenico as plainly, though thinner, poor lad, by much than he was, – as plainly as I now see – Santa Virgine! what is the matter with Nina?"

She had fainted. The company broke up, and she was left to her sister's care. When the poor child came to herself she was fully aware of her situation, and said nothing, except expressing a wish to retire to rest. Maria was in high spirits at the prospect of her long holiday at home; but the illness of her sister made her refrain from talking that night, and blessing her, as she said good-night, she soon slept. Domenico starving! – Domenico trying to escape and dying through hunger, was the vision of horror that wholly possessed poor Anina. At another time, the discovery that her lover was a robber might have inflicted pangs as keen as those which she now felt; but this at present made a faint impression, obscured by worse wretchedness. Maria was in a deep and tranquil sleep. Anina rose, dressed herself silently, and crept downstairs. She stored her market-basket with what food there was in the house, and, unlatching the cottage-door, issued forth, resolved to reach Rocca Giovane, and to administer to her lover's dreadful wants. The night was dark, but this was favourable, for she knew every path and turn of the hills, every bush and knoll of ground between her home and the deserted village which occupies the summit of that hill. You may see the dark outline of some of its houses about two hours' walk from her cottage. The night was dark, but still; the *libeccio* brought the clouds below the mountain-tops, and veiled the horizon in mist; not a leaf stirred; her footsteps sounded loud in her ears, but resolution overcame fear. She had entered yon ilex grove, her spirits rose with her success, when suddenly she was challenged by a sentinel; no time for escape; fear chilled her blood; her basket dropped from her arm; its contents rolled out on the ground; the soldier fired his gun, and brought several others round him; she was made prisoner.

In the morning, when Maria awoke she missed her sister from her side. I have overslept myself, she thought, and Nina would not disturb me. But when she came downstairs and met her father, and Anina did not appear, they began to wonder. She was not in the *podere*; two hours passed, and then Andrea went to seek her. Entering the near village, he saw the contadini crowding together, and a stifled exclamation of "Ecco il padre!" told him that some evil had betided. His first impression was that his daughter was drowned; but the truth, that she had been taken by the French carrying provisions within the forbidden line, was still more terrible. He returned in frantic desperation to his cottage, first to acquaint Maria with what had happened, and then to ascend the hill to save his child from her impending fate. Maria heard his tale with horror; but an hospital is a school in which to learn self-possession and presence of mind. "Do you remain, my father," she said; "I will go. My holy character will awe these men, my tears move them: trust me; I swear that I will save my sister." Andrea yielded to her superior courage and energy.

The nuns of Santa Chiara when out of their convent do not usually wear their monastic habit, but dress simply in a black gown. Maria, however, had brought her nun's habiliments with her, and, thinking thus to impress the soldiers with respect, she now put them on. She received her father's benediction, and, asking that of the Virgin and the saints, she departed on her expedition. Ascending the hill, she was soon stopped by the sentinels. She asked to see their commanding officer, and being conducted to him, she announced herself as the sister of the unfortunate girl who had been captured the night before. The officer, who had received her with carelessness, now changed countenance: his serious look frightened Maria, who clasped her hands, exclaiming, "You have not injured the child! she is safe!"

"She is safe – now," he replied with hesitation; "but there is no hope of pardon."

"Holy Virgin, have mercy on her! What will be done to her?"

"I have received strict orders: in two hours she dies."

"No! no!" exclaimed Maria impetuously, "that cannot be! You cannot be so wicked as to murder a child like her."

"She is old enough, madame," said the officer, "to know that she ought not to disobey orders; mine are so strict, that were she but nine years old, she dies."

These terrible words stung Maria to fresh resolution: she entreated for mercy; she knelt; she vowed that she would not depart without her sister; she appealed to Heaven and the saints. The officer, though cold-hearted, was good-natured and courteous, and he assured her with the utmost gentleness that her supplications were of no avail; that were the criminal his own daughter he must enforce his orders. As a sole concession, he permitted her to see her sister. Despair inspired the nun with energy; she almost ran up the hill, out-speeding her guide: they crossed a folding of the hills to a little sheep-cot, where sentinels paraded before the door. There was no glass to the windows, so the shutters were shut; and when Maria first went in from the bright daylight she hardly saw the slight figure of her sister leaning against the wall, her dark hair fallen below her waist, her head sunk on her bosom, over which her arms were folded. She started wildly as the door opened, saw her sister, and sprang with a piercing shriek into her arms.

They were left alone together: Anina uttered a thousand frantic exclamations, beseeching her sister to save her, and shuddering at the near approach of her fate. Maria had felt herself, since their mother's death, the natural protectress and support of her sister, and she never deemed herself so called on to fulfil this character as now that the trembling girl clasped her neck, – her tears falling on her cheeks, and her choked voice entreating her to save her. The thought – O could I suffer instead of you! was in her heart, and she was about to express it, when it suggested another idea, on which she was resolved to act. First she soothed Anina by her promises, then glanced round the cot; they were quite alone: she went to the window, and through a crevice saw the soldiers conversing at some distance. "Yes, dearest sister," she cried, "I will – I can save you – quick – we must change dresses – there is no time to be lost I – you must escape in my habit."

"And you remain to die?"

"They dare not murder the innocent, a nun! Fear not for me – I am safe."

Anina easily yielded to her sister, but her fingers trembled; every string she touched she entangled. Maria was perfectly self-possessed, pale, but calm. She tied up her sister's long hair, and adjusted her veil over it so as to conceal it; she unlaced her bodice, and arranged the folds of her own habit on her with the greatest care – then more hastily she assumed the dress of her sister, putting on, after a lapse of many years, her native contadina costume. Anina stood by, weeping and help-less, hardly hearing her sister's injunctions to return speedily to their father, and under his guidance to seek sanctuary. The guard now opened the door. Anina clung to her sister in terror, while she, in soothing tones, entreated her to calm herself.

The soldier said they must delay no longer, for the priest had arrived to confess the prisoner.

To Anina the idea of confession associated with death was terrible; to Maria it brought hope. She whispered, in a smothered voice, "The priest will protect me – fear not – hasten to our father!"

Anina almost mechanically obeyed: weeping, with her handkerchief placed unaffectedly before her face, she passed the soldiers; they closed the door on the prisoner, who hastened to the window, and saw her sister descend the hill with tottering steps, till she was lost behind some rising ground. The nun fell on her knees – cold dew bathed her brow, instinctively she feared: the French had shown small respect for the monastic character; they destroyed the convents and desecrated the churches. Would they be merciful to her, and spare the innocent? Alas! was not Anina innocent also? Her sole crime had been disobeying an arbitrary command, and she had done the same.

"Courage!" cried Maria; "perhaps I am fitter to die than my sister is. Gesu, pardon me my sins, but I do not believe that I shall out live this day!"

In the meantime, Anina descended the hill slowly and trembling. She feared discovery, – she feared for her sister, – and above all, at the present moment, she feared the reproaches and anger of her father. By dwelling on this last idea, it became exaggerated into excessive terror, and she determined, instead of returning to her home, to make a circuit among the hills, to find her way by herself to Albano, where she trusted to find protection from her pastor and confessor. She avoided the open paths, and following rather the direction she wished to pursue than any beaten road, she passed along nearer to Rocca Giovane than she anticipated. She looked up at its ruined houses and bell-less steeple, straining her eyes to catch a glimpse of him, the author of all her ills. A low but distinct whistle reached her ear, not far off; she started, – she remembered that on the night when she last saw Domenico a note like that had called him from her side; the sound was echoed and re-echoed from other quarters; she stood aghast, her bosom heaving, her hands clasped. First she saw a dark and ragged head of hair, shadowing two fiercely gleaming eyes, rise from beneath a bush. She screamed, but before she could repeat her scream three men leapt from behind a rock, secured her arms, threw a cloth over her face, and hurried her up the acclivity. Their talk, as she went along, informed her of the horror and danger of her situation.

Pity, they said, that the holy father and some of his red stockings did not command the troops: with a nun in their hands, they might obtain any terms. Coarse jests passed as they dragged their victim towards their ruined village. The paving of the street told her when they arrived at Rocca Giovane, and the change of atmosphere that they entered a house. They unbandaged her eyes: the scene was squalid and miserable, the walls ragged and black with smoke, the floor strewn with offals and dirt; a rude table and broken bench was all the furniture; and the leaves of Indian corn, heaped high in one corner, served, it seemed, for a bed, for a man lay on it, his head buried in his folded arms. Anina looked round on her savage hosts: their countenances expressed every variety of brutal ferocity, now rendered more dreadful from gaunt famine and suffering.

"Oh, there is none who will save me!" she cried. The voice startled the man who was lying on the floor; he lept up – it was Domenico: Domenico, so changed, with sunk cheeks and eyes, matted hair, and looks whose wildness and desperation differed little from the dark countenances around him. Could this be her lover?

His recognition and surprise at her dress led to an explanation. When the robbers first heard that their prey was no prize, they were mortified and angry; but when she related the danger she had incurred by endeavouring to bring them food, they swore with horrid oaths that no harm should befall her, but that if she liked she might make one of them in all honour and equality. The innocent girl shuddered. "Let me go," she cried; "let me only escape and hide myself in a convent for ever!"

Domenico looked at her in agony. "Yes, poor child," he

said; "go save yourself: God grant no evil befall you; the ruin is too wide already." Then turning eagerly to his comrades, he continued: "You hear her story. She was to have been shot for bringing food to us: her sister has substituted herself in her place. We know the French; one victim is to them as good as another: Maria dies in their hands. Let us save her. Our time is up; we must fall like men, or starve like dogs: we have still ammunition, still some strength left. To arms! let us rush on the poltroons, free their prisoner, and escape or die!"

There needed but an impulse like this to urge the outlaws to desperate resolves. They prepared their arms with looks of ferocious determination. Domenico, meanwhile, led Anina out of the house, to the verge of the hill, inquiring whether she intended to go. On her saying to Albano, he observed, "That were hardly safe; be guided by me, I entreat you: take these piastres, hire the first conveyance you find, hasten to Rome, to the convent of Santa Chiara: for pity's sake, do not linger in this neighbourhood."

"I will obey your injunctions, Domenico," she replied, "but I cannot take your money; it has cost you too dear: fear not, I shall arrive safely at Rome without that ill-fated silver."

Domenico's comrades now called loudly to him: he had no time to urge his request; he threw the despised dollars at her feet.

"Nina, adieu for ever," he said: "may you love again more happily!"

"Never!" she replied. "God has saved me in this dress; it were sacrilege to change it: I shall never quit Santa Chiara."

Domenico had led her a part of the way down the rock; his comrades appeared at the top, calling to him.

"Gesu save you!" cried he: "reach the convent – Maria shall join you there before night. Farewell!" He hastily kissed her hand, and sprang up the acclivity to rejoin his impatient friends.

The unfortunate Andrea had waited long for the return of his children. The leafless trees and bright clear atmosphere permitted every object to be visible, but he saw no trace of them on the hill-side; the shadows of the dial showed noon to be passed, when, with uncontrollable impatience, he began to climb the hill, towards the spot where Anina had been taken. The path he pursued was in part the same that this unhappy girl had taken on her way to Rome. The father and daughter met: the old man saw the nun's dress, and saw her unaccompanied: she covered her face with her hands in a transport of fear and shame; but when, mistaking her for Maria, he asked in a tone of anguish for his youngest darling, her arms fell – she dared not raise her eyes, which streamed with tears.

"Unhappy girl!" exclaimed Andrea, "where is your sister?"

She pointed to the cottage prison, now discernible near the summit of a steep acclivity. "She is safe," she replied: "she saved me; but they dare not murder her."

"Heaven bless her for this good deed!" exclaimed the old man fervently; "but you hasten on your way, and I will go in search of her."

Each proceeded on an opposite path. The old man wound up the hill, now in view, and now losing sight of the hut where his child was captive: he was aged, and the way was steep. Once, when the closing of the hill hid the point towards which he for ever strained his eyes, a single shot was fired in that direction: his staff fell from his hands, his knees trembled and failed him; several minutes of dead silence elapsed before he recovered himself sufficiently to proceed: full of fears he went on, and at the next turn saw the cot again. A party of soldiers were on the open space before it, drawn up in a line as if expecting an attack. In a few moments from above them shots were fired, which they returned, and the whole was enveloped and veiled in smoke. Still Andrea climbed the hill, eager to discover what had become of his child: the firing continued quick and hot. Now and then, in the pauses of musketry and the answering echoes of the mountains, he heard a funeral chant; presently, before he was aware, at a turning of the hill, he met a company of priests and contadini, carrying a large cross and a bier. The miserable father rushed forward with frantic impatience; the awe-struck peasants set down their load – the face was uncovered, and the wretched man fell helpless on the corpse of his murdered child.

The Countess Atanasia paused, overcome by the emotions inspired by the history she related. A long pause ensued: at length one of the party observed, "Maria, then, was the sacrifice to her goodness."

"The French," said the countess, "did not venerate her holy vocation; one peasant girl to them was the same as another. The immolation of any victim suited their purpose of awe-striking the peasantry. Scarcely, however, had the shot entered her heart, and her blameless spirit been received by the saints in Paradise, when Domenico and his followers rushed down the hill to avenge her and themselves. The contest was furious and bloody; twenty French soldiers fell, and not one of the banditti escaped, – Domenico, the foremost of the assailants, being the first to fall."

I asked, "And where are now Anina and her father?"

"You may see them, if you will," said the countess, "on your return to Rome. She is a nun of Santa Chiara. Constant acts of benevolence and piety have inspired her with calm and resignation. Her prayers are daily put up for Domenico's soul, and she hopes, through the intercession of the Virgin, to rejoin him in the other world.

"Andrea is very old; he has outlived the memory of his sufferings; but he derives comfort from the filial attentions of his surviving daughter. But when I look at his cottage on this lake, and remember the happy laughing face of Anina among the vines, I shudder at the recollection of the passion that has made her cheeks pale, her thoughts for ever conversant with death, her only wish to find repose in the grave."

EUPHRASIA

A Tale Of Greece

It was not long after the breaking out of the Greek Revolution that Harry Valency visited Greece. Many an Englishman was led thither at that time by the spirit of adventure, and many perished. Valency was not nineteen; his spirit was wild and reckless; – thought or care had never touched his brow; his heart was too light for love. Restless and energetic, he longed to try his powers, with the instinct that leads the young deer to butt against trees, or to wrestle with each other in the forest-dells. He was the only son of a widowed mother, whose life was wrapped in his, and he loved her fondly; yet left her, impelled by a desire for adventure, unable to understand what anxiety and fear meant; and in his own person eager to meet even misfortune, so that it came in a guise to call forth manly and active struggles. He longed to have the pages of his young life written over by deeds that would hereafter be memories, to which he could turn with delight. The cause of Greece warmed his soul. He was in a transport of ecstasy when he touched the shores of that antique land, and looked around on mountain and mountain-stream, whose names were associated with the most heroic acts, and the most sublime poetry man ever achieved or wrote. Yes, he was now in Greece. He was about to fight in her cause against the usurping Turk. He had prepared himself by a sedulous study of Romaic; he was on his way to the seat of Government, to offer his services. To proceed thither from the spot where he had disembarked was a matter of some difficulty; the Turkish troops being then in possession of many of the passes. At length he heard that a band of about fifty Greek soldiers, headed by a young but brave and renowned chief, was about to pursue the same road; he asked, and obtained leave to accompany them.

How delightful was the commencement of the journey! How beautiful the country – defile and steep hill-side, by which they proceeded; where the grey olive clothed the upland, or vines, embracing elms, red now with late summer tints, varied the scene. The mountain-tops were bare, or crowned with pines, and torrents ran down the sides and fed a stream in the dell. The air was balmy; the cicada loud and merry – to live was to be happy. Valency was mounted on a spirited horse; he made it leap and caracole. He threw a spear against a tree, and dashed after to recover it. He fired at a mark as he hurried on at full gallop; every feat was insufficient to tame his exhaustless spirits.

The chief marked him with eyes, whose deep melancholy expression darkened as he gazed. He was known as bravest among the brave; yet gentle as a woman. He was young and singularly handsome; his countenance was stamped with traces of intellectual refinement, while his person was tall, muscular, and strong, but so gracefully formed, that every attitude reminded you of some Praxitilean shape of his own native land. Once he had been more beautiful; joy, as well as tenderness, and a soldier's ardour had lighted up his dark eye; his lip had been the home of smiles, and the thoughts, which presided in his brow, had been as clear and soft and gladsome as that godlike brow itself. Now this was changed. Grief had become a master passion: his cheeks were sunken; his eye seemed to brood eternally over melancholy regrets; his measured harmonious voice was attuned to the utterance of no light fancy or gay sallies; he spoke only the necessary words of direction to his followers, and then silence and gloom gathered over his face. His sorrow was respected; for it was known to be well founded, and to spring from a recent disaster. If any of his troop desired to indulge in merriment, they withdrew from his vicinity. It was strange to them to hear the light laugh of the English youth ring through the grove, and to catch the tones of his merry voice, as he sang some of their own gayest songs. The chief gazed with interest. There was a winning frankness in the boy; he was so very young, and all he did was in graceful accordance with his age. We are alike mere youths, thought the chief, and how different! Yet soon he may become like me. He soars like an eagle; but the eagle may be wounded, and stoop to earth; because earth contains its secret and its regret.

Suddenly Valency, who was some hundred yards in advance, was encountered by a Greek, riding at full speed towards the advancing troop.

"Back! back! silence!" the man cried. He was a scout, who had been sent on before, and now brought tidings that a troop of three or four hundred of the Turkish army were entering the defile, and would soon advance on the handful of men which Valency accompanied. The scout rode directly up to the leader, and made his report, adding,—

"We have yet time. If we fall back but a quarter of a mile, there is a path I know, by which I can guide you across the mountain; on the other side we shall be safe."

A smile of scorn for a moment wreathed the lip of the chief at the word safety, but his face soon reassumed its usual sad composure. The troop had halted; each man bent his eye on the leader. Valency, in particular, marked the look of scorn, and felt that he would never retreat before danger.

"Comrades!" the chief thus addressed his men, "it shall never be said that Greeks fell back to make way for the destroyers; we will betake ourselves to our old warfare. Before we entered this olive wood, we passed a thick cover, where the dark jutting mountain-side threw a deep shadow across our path, and the torrent drowned all sound of voice or hoof. There we shall find ambush; there the enemy will meet death."

He turned his horse's head, and in a few minutes reached the spot he named; the men were mostly eager for the fray – while one or two eyed the mountain-side, and then the path that led to the village, which they had quitted that morning. The chief saw their look, and he glanced also at the English youth, who had thrown himself from his horse, and was busy loading and priming his arms. The chief rode up to him.

"You are our guest and fellow-traveller," he said, "but not our comrade in the fight. We are about to meet danger – it may be that not one of us shall escape. You have no injuries to avenge, no liberty to gain; you have friends – probably a mother – in your native land. You must not fall with us. I am going to send a message to warn the village we last passed through – do you accompany my messengers."

Valency had listened attentively at first; but as the chief continued, his attention reverted to his task of loading his pistols. The last words called a blush into his cheek.

"You treat me as a boy," he cried; "I may be one in aspect, but you shall find me a man in heart this day. You also young, I have not deserved your scorn!"

The chief caught the youth's flashing eye. He held out his hand to him, saying, "Forgive me."

"I will," said Valency, "on one condition; give me a post of danger – of honour. You owe it to me in reparation of the insult you offered."

"Be it so," said the chief; "your place shall be at my side."

A few minutes more and his dispositions were made; – two of the most down-hearted of the troop were despatched to alarm the village, the rest were placed behind the rocks; beneath the bushes, wherever broken ground, or tuft of underwood, or fragment from the cliff, afforded shelter and concealment, a man was placed; while the chief himself took his stand on an elevated platform, and, sheltered by a tree, gazed upon the road. Soon the tramp of horses, the busy sound of feet and voices were heard, overpowering the rushing of the stream; and turban and musket could be distinguished as the enemy's troop threaded the defile.

The shout of battle – the firing – the clash of weapons were over. Above the crest of the hill, whose side had afforded ambush to the Greeks, the crescent moon hung, just about to dip behind; the stars in her train burnt bright as lamps floating in the firmament; while the fire-flies flashed among the myrtle underwood and up the mountain-side; and sometimes the steel of the arms strewn around, dropped from the hand of the dead, caught and reflected the flashes of the celestial or earthly stars. The ground was strewn with the slain. Such of the enemy as had cut their way through were already far – the sound of their horses' hoofs had died away. The Greeks who had fled across the mountain had reached a place of safety – none lay there but the silent dead – cold as the moonbeam that rested for a moment on their pale faces. All were still and motionless; some lay on the hill-side among the underwood – some on the open road – horses and men had fallen, pell mell – none moved – none breathed.

Yet there was a sigh – it was lost in the murmur of the stream; a groan succeeded, and then a voice feeble and bro-ken, "My mother, my poor mother!" – the pale lips that spoke these words could form no other, a gush of tears followed. The cry seemed to awake another form from among the dead. One of the prostrate bodies raised itself slowly and painfully on its arm, the eyes were filmy, the countenance pallid from approaching death, the voice was hollow, yet firm, that said, "Who speaks? – who lives? – who weeps?"

The question struck shame to the wounded man; he checked his overflow of passionate sobbings. The other spoke again, "It was not the voice of a Greek – yet I thought I had saved that gallant boy – the ball meant for him is now in my side. – Speak again, young Englishman – on whom do you call?"

"On her who will weep my death too bitterly – on my

mother," replied Valency, and tears would follow the loved name.

"Art thou wounded to death?" asked the chief.

"Thus unaided I must die," he replied; "yet, could I reach those waters, I might live – I must try." And Valency rose; he staggered a few steps, and fell heavily at the feet of the chief. He had fainted. The Greek looked on the ghastly pallor of his face; he half rose – his own wound did not bleed, but it was mortal, and a deadly sickness had gathered round his heart, and chilled his brow, which he strove to master, that he might save the English boy. The effort brought cold drops on his brow, as he rose on his knees and stooped to raise the head of Valency; he shuddered to feel the warm moisture his hand encountered. It is his blood; his life-blood he thought; and again he placed his head on the earth, and continued a moment still, summoning what vitality remained to him to animate his limbs. Then with a determined effort he rose, and staggered to the banks of the stream. He held a steel cap in his hand – and now he stooped down to fill it; but with the effort the ground slid from under him, and he fell. There was a ringing in his ears – a cold dew on his brow – his breath came thick – the cap had fallen from his hand – he was dying. The bough of a tree, shot off in the morning's melée, lay near; – the mind, even of a dying man, can form swift, unerring combinations of thought; – it was his last chance – the bough was plunged in the waters, and he scattered the grateful, reviving drops over his face; vigour returned with the act, and he could stoop and fill the cap, and drink a deep draught, which for a moment restored the vital powers. And now he carried water to Valency; he dipped the unfolded turban of a Turk in the stream, and bound the youth's wound, which was a deep sabre cut in the shoulder, that had bled copiously. Valency revived – life gathered warm in his heart – his cheeks, though still pale, lost the ashy hue of death – his limbs again seemed willing to obey his will – he sat up, but he was too weak, and his head dropped. As a mother tending her sick first-born, the Greek chief hovered over him; he brought a cloak to pillow his head; as he picked up this, he found that some careful soldier had brought a small bag at his saddle-bow, in which was a loaf and a bunch or two of grapes; he gave them to the youth, who ate. Valency now recognised his saviour; at first he wondered to see him there, tending on him, apparently unhurt; but soon the chief sank to the ground, and Valency could mark the rigidity of feature, and ghastliness of aspect, that portended death. In his turn he would have assisted his friend; but the chief stopped him – "You die if you move," he said; "your wound will bleed afresh, and you will die, while you cannot aid me. My weakness does not arise from mere loss of blood. The messenger of death has reached a vital part – yet a little while and the soul will obey the summons. It is slow, slow is the deliverance; yet the long creeping hour will come at last, and I shall be free."

"Do not speak thus," cried Valency; "I am strong now – I will go for help."

"There is no help for me," replied the chief, "save the death I desire. I command you, move not."

Valency had risen, but the effort was vain: his knees bent under him, his head spun round; before he could save himself he had sunk to the ground.

"Why torture yourself?" said the chief. "A few hours and help will come: it will not injure you to pass this interval beneath this calm sky. The cowards who fled will alarm the country; by dawn succour will be here: you must wait for it. I too must wait – not for help, but for death. It is soothing even to me to die here beneath this sky, with the murmurs of yonder stream in my ear, the shadows of my native mountains thrown athwart. Could aught save me, it would be the balmy airs of this most blessed night; my soul feels the bliss, though my body is sick and fast stiffening in death. Such was not the hour when she died whom soon I shall meet, my Euphrasia, my own sweet sister, in heaven!"

It was strange, Valency said, that at such an hour, but half saved from death, and his preserver in the grim destroyer's clutches, that he should feel curiosity to know the Greek chief's story. His youth, his beauty, his valour – the act, which Valency well remembered, of his springing forward so as to shield him with his own person – his last words and thoughts devoted to the soft recollection of a beloved sister, – awakened an interest beyond even the present hour, fraught as it was with the chances of life and death. He questioned the chief. Probably fever had succeeded to his previous state of weakness, imparted a deceitful strength, and even inclined him to talk; for thus dying, unaided and unsheltered, with the starry sky overhead, he willingly reverted to the years of his youth and to the miserable event which a few months before had eclipsed the sun of his life and rendered death welcome.

They – brother and sister, Constantine and Euphrasia – were the last of their race. They were orphans; their youth was passed under the guardianship of the brother by adoption of their father, whom they named father, and who loved them. He was a glorious old man, nursed in classic lore, and more familiar with the deeds of men who had glorified his country several thousand years before than with any more modern names. Yet all who had ever done and suffered for Greece were embalmed in his memory, and honoured as martyrs in the best of causes. He had been educated in Paris, and travelled in Europe and America, and was aware of the progress made in the science of politics all over the civilised world. He felt that Greece would soon share the benefits to arise from the changes then operating, and he looked forward at no distant day to its liberation from bondage. He educated his young ward for that day. Had he believed that Greece would have continued hopelessly enslaved, he had brought him up as a scholar and a recluse: but, assured of the impending struggle, he made him a warrior; he implanted a detestation of the oppressor, a yearning love for the sacred blessings of freedom, a noble desire to have his name enrolled among the deliverers of his country. The education he bestowed on Euphrasia was yet more singular. He knew that though liberty must be bought and maintained by the sword, yet that its dearest blessings must be derived from civilisation and knowledge; and he believed women to be the proper fosterers of these. They cannot handle a sword nor endure bodily labour for their country, but they could refine the manners, exalt the souls – impart honour, and truth, and wisdom to their relatives and their children. Euphrasia, therefore, he made a scholar. By nature she was an enthusiast and a poet. The study of the classic literature of her country corrected her taste and exalted her love of the beautiful. While a child, she improvised passionate songs of liberty; and as she grew in years and loveliness, and her heart opened to tenderness, and she became aware of all the honour and happiness that a woman must derive from being held the friend of man, not his slave, she thanked God that she was a Greek and a Christian; and holding fast by the advantages which these names conferred, she looked forward eagerly to the day when Mohammedanism should no longer contaminate her native land, and when her countrywomen should be awakened from ignorance and sloth in which they were plunged, and learn that their proper vocation in the creation was that of mothers of heroes and teachers of sages.

Her brother was her idol, her hope, her joy. And he who had been taught that his career must be that of deeds, not words, yet was fired by her poetry and eloquence to desire glory yet more eagerly, and to devote himself yet more entirely and with purer ardour to the hope of one day living and dying for his country. The first sorrow the orphans knew was the death of their adopted father. He descended to the grave full of years and honour. Constantine was then eighteen; his fair sister had just entered her fifteenth year. Often they spent the night beside the revered tomb of their lost friend, talking of the hopes and aspirations he had implanted. The young can form such sublime, such beautiful dreams. No disappointment, no evil, no bad passion shadows their glorious visions. To dare and do greatly for Greece was the ambition of Constantine. To cheer and watch over her brother, to regulate his wilder and more untaught soul, to paint in celestial colours the bourne he tended towards by action, were Euphrasia's tasks.

"There is a heaven," said the dying man as he told his tale, – "there is a paradise for those who die in the just cause. I know not what joys are there prepared for the blest; but they can scarcely transcend those that were mine as I listened to my own sweet sister, and felt my heart swell with patriotism and fond, warm affection."

At length there was a stir through the land, and Constantine made a journey of some distance, to confer with the capitani of the mountains, and to prepare for the outbreak of the revolution. The moment came, sooner even than he expected. As an eagle chained when the iron links drop from him, and with clang of wing and bright undazzled eye he soars to heaven, so did Constantine feel when freedom to Greece became the war-cry. He was still among the mountains when first the echoes of his native valleys repeated that animating, that sacred word. Instead of returning, as he intended, to his Athenian home, he was hurried off to Western Greece, and became a participator in a series of warlike movements, the promised success of which filled him with transport.

Suddenly a pause came in the delirium of joy which possessed his soul. He received not the accustomed letters from his sister – missives which had been to him angelic messengers, teaching him patience with the unworthy – hope in disappointment – certainty of final triumph. Those dear letters ceased; and he thought he saw in the countenances of his friends around a concealed knowledge of evil. He questioned them: their answers were evasive. At the same time, they endeavoured to fill his mind with the details of some anticipated exploit in which his presence and co-operation was necessary. Day after day passed; he could not leave his post without injury to the cause, without even the taint of dishonour. He belonged to a band of Albanians, by whom he had been received as a brother and he could not desert them in the hour of danger. But the suspense grew too terrible; and at length, finding that there was an interval of a few days which he might call his own, he left the camp, resting neither day nor night; dismounting from one horse only to bestride another, in forty-eight hours he was in Athens, before his vacant, desecrated home. The tale of horror was soon told. Athens was still in the hands of the Turks; the sister of a rebel had become the prey of the oppressor. She had none to guard her. Her matchless beauty had been seen and marked by the son of the pasha; she had for the last two months been immured in his harem.

"Despair is a cold, dark feeling," said the dying warrior; "if I may name that despair which had a hope – a certainty – an aim. Had Euphrasia died I had wept. Now my eyes were horn – my heart stone. I was silent. I neither expressed resentment nor revenge. I concealed myself by day; at night I wandered round the tyrant's dwelling. It was a pleasure-palace, one of the most luxurious in our beloved Athens. At this time it was carefully guarded: my character was known, and Euphrasia's worth; and the oppressor feared the result of his deed. Still, under shadow of darkness I drew near. I marked the position of the women's apartments – I learned the number – the length of the watch – the orders they received, and then I returned to the camp. I revealed my project to a few select spirits. They were fired by my wrongs, and eager to deliver my Euphrasia."—

Constantine broke off – a spasm of pain shook his body. After this had passed he lay motionless for a few minutes; then starting up, as fever and delirium, excited by the exertion of speaking, increased by the agonies of recollection, at last fully possessed him. "What is this?" he cried. "Fire! Yes, the palace burns. Do you not hear the roaring of the flames, and thunder too – the artillery of Heaven levelled against the unblest? Ha! a shot – he falls – they are driven back – now fling the torches – the wood crackles – there, there are the women's rooms – ha! poor victims! lo! you shudder and fly! Fear not; give me only my Euphrasia! – my own Euphrasia! No disguise can hide thee, dressed as a Turkish bride crowned with flowers, thy lovely face, the seat of unutterable woe – still, my sweet sister, even in this smoke and tumult of this house, thou art the angel of my life! Spring into my arms, poor, frightened bird; cling to me – it is herself – her voice – her fair arms are round my neck – what ruin – what flame – what choking smoke – what driving storm can stay me? Soft! the burning breach is passed – there are steps – gently – dear one, I am firm – fear not! – what eyes glare? – fear not, Euphrasia, he is dead – the miserable retainers of the tyrant fell beneath our onset – ha! a shot – gracious Panagia, is this thy protection?" Thus did he continue to rave: the onset, the burning of the palace, the deliverance of his sister, all seemed to pass again vividly as if in present action. His eyes glared; he tossed up his arms; he shouted as if calling his followers around him; and then in tones of heartfelt tenderness he addressed the fair burden he fancied that he bore – till, with a shriek, he cried again, "A shot!" and sank to the ground as if his heartstrings had broken.

An interval of calm succeeded; he was exhausted; his voice was broken.

"What have I told thee?" he continued feebly; "I have said how a mere handful of men attacked the palace, and drove back the guards – how we strove in vain to make good our entrance – fresh troops were on their way – there was no alternative; we fired the palace. Deep in the seclusion of the harem the women had retreated, a herd of frightened deer. One alone stood erect. Her eyes bent on the intruders – a dagger in her hand – majestic and fearless, her face was marked with traces of passed suffering, but at the moment the stern resolution her soft features expressed was more than human. The moment she saw me, all was changed; the angel alone beamed in her countenance. Her dagger fell from her hand – she was in my arms – I bore her from the burning roof – the rest you know; have I not said it? Some miscreant, who survived the slaughter, and yet lay as dead on the earth, aimed a deadly shot. She did not shriek. At first she clung closer to my neck, and then I felt her frame shiver in my arms and her hold relax. I trusted that fear alone moved her; but she knew not fear – it was death. Horses had been prepared, and were waiting; a few hours more and I hoped to be on our way to the west, to that portion of Greece that was free. But I felt her head fall on my shoulder. I heard her whisper, 'I die, my brother! carry me to our father's tomb.'

"My soul yearned to comply with her request; but it was impossible. The city was alarmed; troops gathering from all quarters. Our safety lay in flight, for still I thought that her wound was not mortal. I bore her to the spot where we had left our horses. Here two or three of my comrades speedily joined me; they had rescued the women of the harem from the flames, but the various sounds denoting the advance of the Turkish soldiery caused them to hurry from the scene. I leapt on my horse, and placed my sweet sister before me, and we fled amain through desert streets, I well knew how to choose, and along the lanes of the suburbs into the open country, where, deviating from the high-road, along which I directed my companions to proceed in all haste – alone with my beloved burden, I sought a solitary, unsuspected spot among the neighbouring hills. The storm which had ceased for a time, now broke afresh; the deafening thunder drowned every other sound, while the frequent glare of the lightning showed us our path; my horse did not quail before it. Euphrasia still lay clinging to me; no complaint escaped her; a few words of fondness, of encouragement, of pious resignation, she now and then breathed forth. I knew not she was dying, till at last entering a retired valley, where an olive wood afforded shelter, and still better the portico of a fallen ancient temple, I dismounted and bore her to the marble steps, on which I placed her. Then indeed I felt how near the beloved one was to death, from which I could not save her. The lightning showed me her face – pale as the marble which pillowed it. Her dress was dabbled in warm blood, which soon stained the stones on which she lay. I took her hand; it was deathly cold. I raised her from the marble; I pillowed her cheek upon my heart. I repressed my despair, or rather my despair in that hour was mild and soft as herself. There was no help – no hope. The life-blood oozed fast from her side; scarce could she raise her heavy eyelids to look on me; her voice could no longer articulate my name. The burden of her fair limbs grew heavier and more chill; soon it was a corpse only that I held. When I knew that her sufferings were over, I raised her once more in my arms, and once more I placed her before me on my horse, and betook me to my journey. The storm was over now, and the moon bright above. Earth glittered under the rays, and a soft breeze swept by, as if heaven itself became clear and peaceful to receive her stainless soul, and present it to its Maker. By morning's dawn, I stopped at a convent gate, and rang. To the holy maidens within I consigned my own fair Euphrasia. I kissed but once again her dear brow, which spoke of peace in death; and then saw her placed upon a bier, and was away, back to my camp, to live and die for Greece."

He grew more silent as he became weaker. Now and then he spoke a few words to record some other of Euphrasia's perfections, or to repeat some of her dying words; to speak of her magnanimity, her genius, her love, and his own wish to die.

"I might have lived," he said, "till her image had faded in my mind, or been mingled with less holy memories. I die young, all her own."

His voice grew more feeble after this; he complained of cold. Valency continued: "I contrived to rise, and crawl about, and to collect a capote or two, and a pelisse from among the slain, with some of which I covered him; and then I drew one over myself, for the air grew chill, as midnight had passed away and the morning hour drew near. The warmth which the coverings imparted calmed the aching of my wound, and, strange to say, I felt slumber creep over me. I tried to watch and wake. At first the stars above and the dark forms of the mountains mingled with my dreamy feelings; but soon I lost all sense of where I was, and what I had suffered, and slept peacefully and long.

"The morning sunbeams, as creeping down the hill-side they at last fell upon my face, awoke me. At first I had forgotten all thought of the events of the past night, and my first impulse was to spring up, crying aloud, where am I? but the stiffness of my limbs and their weakness, soon revealed the truth. Gladly I now welcomed the sound of voices, and marked the approach of a number of peasants along the ravine. Hitherto, strange to say, I had thought only of myself; but with the ideas of succour came the recollection of my companion, and the tale of the previous night. I glanced eagerly to where he lay; his posture disclosed his state; he was still, and stiff, and dead. Yet his countenance was calm and beautiful. He had died in the dear hope of meeting his sister, and her image had shed peace over the last moment of life.

"I am ashamed to revert to myself. The death of Constantine is the true end of my tale. My wound was a severe one. I was forced to leave Greece, and for some months remained between life and death in Cefalonia, till a good constitution saved me, when at once I returned to England."

The Dream

"Chi dice mal d'amore
Dice una falsità!"

– Italian Song.

The time of the occurrence of the little legend about to be narrated, was that of the commencement of the reign of Henry IV. of France, whose accession and conversion, while they brought peace to the kingdom whose throne he ascended, were inadequate to heal the deep wounds mutually inflicted by the inimical parties. Private feuds, and the memory of mortal injuries, existed between those now apparently united; and often did the hands that had clasped each other in seeming friendly greeting, involuntarily, as the grasp was released, clasp the dagger's hilt, as fitter spokesman to their passions than the words of courtesy that had just fallen from their lips. Many of the fiercer Catholics retreated to their distant provinces; and while they concealed in solitude their rankling discontent, not less keenly did they long for the day when they might show it openly.

In a large and fortified chateau built on a rugged steep overlooking the Loire, not far from the town of Nantes, dwelt the last of her race, and the heiress of their fortunes, the young and beautiful Countess de Villeneuve. She had spent the preceding year in complete solitude in her secluded abode; and the mourning she wore for a father and two brothers, the victims of the civil wars, was a graceful and good reason why she did not appear at court, and mingle with its festivities. But the orphan countess inherited a high name and broad lands; and it was soon signified to her that the king, her guardian, desired that she should bestow them, together with her hand, upon some noble whose birth and accomplishments should entitle him to the gift. Constance, in reply, expressed her intention of taking vows, and retiring to a convent. The king earnestly and resolutely forbade this act, believing such an idea to be the result of sensibility overwrought by sorrow, and relying on the hope that, after a time, the genial spirit of youth would break through this cloud.

A year passed, and still the countess persisted; and at last Henry, unwilling to exercise compulsion, – desirous, too, of judging for himself of the motives that led one so beautiful, young, and gifted with fortune's favours, to desire to bury herself in a cloister, – announced his intention, now that the period of her mourning was expired, of visiting her chateau; and if he brought not with him, the monarch said, inducement sufficient to change her design, he would yield his consent to its fulfilment.

Many a sad hour had Constance passed – many a day of tears, and many a night of restless misery. She had closed her gates against every visitant; and, like the Lady Olivia in "Twelfth Night," vowed herself to loneliness and weeping. Mistress of herself, she easily silenced the entreaties and remonstrances of underlings, and nursed her grief as it had been the thing she loved. Yet it was too keen, too bitter, too burning, to be a favoured guest. In fact, Constance, young, ardent, and vivacious, battled with it, struggled, and longed to cast it off; but all that was joyful in itself, or fair in outward show, only served to renew it; and she could best support the burden of her sorrow with patience, when, yielding to it, it oppressed but did not torture her.

Constance had left the castle to wander in the neighbouring grounds. Lofty and extensive as were the apartments of her abode, she felt pent up within their walls, beneath their fretted

131

roofs. The spreading uplands and the antique wood, associated to her with every dear recollection of her past life, enticed her to spend hours and days beneath their leafy coverts. The motion and change eternally working, as the wind stirred among the boughs, or the journeying sun rained its beams through them, soothed and called her out of that dull sorrow which clutched her heart with so unrelenting a pang beneath her castle roof.

There was one spot on the verge of the well-wooded park, one nook of ground, whence she could discern the country extended beyond, yet which was in itself thick set with tall umbrageous trees – a spot which she had forsworn, yet whither unconsciously her steps for ever tended, and where now again, for the twentieth time that day, she had unaware found herself. She sat upon a grassy mound, and looked wistfully on the flowers she had herself planted to adorn the verdurous recess – to her the temple of memory and love. She held the letter from the king which was the parent to her of so much despair. Dejection sat upon her features, and her gentle heart asked fate why, so young, unprotected, and forsaken, she should have to struggle with this new form of wretchedness.

"I but ask," she thought, "to live in my father's halls – in the spot familiar to my infancy – to water with my frequent tears the graves of those I loved; and here in these woods, where such a mad dream of happiness was mine, to celebrate for ever the obsequies of Hope!"

A rustling among the boughs now met her ear – her heart beat quick – all again was still.

"Foolish girl!" she half muttered; "dupe of thine own passionate fancy: because here we met; because seated here I have expected, and sounds like these have announced, his dear approach; so now every coney as it stirs, and every bird as it awakens silence, speaks of him. O Gaspar! – mine once – never again will this beloved spot be made glad by thee – never more!"

Again the bushes were stirred, and footsteps were heard in the brake. She rose; her heart beat high; it must be that silly Manon, with her impertinent entreaties for her to return. But the steps were firmer and slower than would be those of her waiting-woman; and now emerging from the shade, she too plainly discerned the intruder. Her first impulse was to fly: – but once again to see him – to hear his voice: – once again before she placed eternal vows between them, to stand together, and find the wide chasm filled which absence had made, could not injure the dead, and would soften the fatal sorrow that made her cheek so pale.

And now he was before her, the same beloved one with whom she had exchanged vows of constancy. He, like her, seemed sad; nor could she resist the imploring glance that entreated her for one moment to remain.

"I come, lady," said the young knight, "without a hope to bend your inflexible will. I come but once again to see you, and to bid you farewell before I depart for the Holy Land. I come to beseech you not to immure yourself in the dark cloister to avoid one as hateful as myself, – one you will never see more. Whether I die or live, France and I are parted for ever!"

"That were fearful, were it true," said Constance; "but King Henry will never so lose his favourite cavalier. The throne you helped to build, you still will guard. Nay, as I ever had power over thought of thine, go not to Palestine."

"One word of yours could detain me – one smile – Constance" – and the youthful lover knelt before her; but her harsher purpose was recalled by the image once so dear and familiar, now so strange and so forbidden.

"Linger no longer here!" she cried. "No smile, no word of mine will ever again be yours. Why are you here – here, where the spirits of the dead wander, and, claiming these shades as their own, curse the false girl who permits their murderer to disturb their sacred repose?"

"When love was young and you were kind," replied the knight, "you taught me to thread the intricacies of these woods – you welcomed me to this dear spot, where once you vowed to be my own – even beneath these ancient trees."

"A wicked sin it was," said Constance, "to unbar my father's doors to the son of his enemy, and dearly is it punished!"

The young knight gained courage as she spoke; yet he dared not move, lest she, who, every instant, appeared ready to take flight, should be startled from her momentary tranquillity; but he slowly replied: – "Those were happy days, Constance, full of terror and deep joy, when evening brought me to your feet; and while hate and vengeance were as its atmosphere to yonder frowning castle, this leafy, starlit bower was the shrine of love."

"Happy? – miserable days!" echoed Constance; "when I imagined good could arise from failing in my duty, and that disobedience would be rewarded of God. Speak not of love, Gaspar! – a sea of blood divides us for ever! Approach me not! The dead and the beloved stand even now between us: their pale shadows warn me of my fault, and menace me for listening to their murderer."

"That am not I!" exclaimed the youth. "Behold, Constance, we are each the last of our race. Death has dealt cruelly with us, and we are alone. It was not so when first we loved – when parent, kinsman, brother, nay, my own mother breathed curses on the house of Villeneuve; and in spite of all I blessed it. I saw thee, my lovely one, and blessed it. The God of peace planted love in our hearts, and with mystery and secrecy we met during many a summer night in the moonlit dells; and when daylight was abroad, in this sweet recess we fled to avoid its scrutiny, and here, even here, where now I kneel in supplication, we both knelt and made our vows. Shall they be broken?"

Constance wept as her lover recalled the images of happy hours. "Never," she exclaimed, "O never! Thou knowest, or wilt soon know, Gaspar, the faith and resolves of one who dare not be yours. Was it for us to talk of love and happiness, when war, and hate, and blood were raging around? The fleeting flowers our young hands strewed were trampled by the deadly encounter of mortal foes. By your father's hand mine died; and little boots it to know whether, as my brother swore, and you deny, your hand did or did not deal the blow that destroyed him. You fought among those by whom he died. Say no more – no other word: it is impiety towards the unreposing dead to hear you. Go, Gaspar; forget me. Under the chivalrous and gallant Henry your career may be glorious; and some fair girl will listen, as once I did, to your vows, and be made happy by them. Farewell! May the Virgin bless you! In my cell and cloister-home I will not forget the best Christian lesson – to pray for our enemies. Gaspar, farewell!"

She glided hastily from the bower: with swift steps she threaded the glade and sought the castle. Once within the seclusion of her own apartment she gave way to the burst of grief that tore her gentle bosom like a tempest; for hers was that worst sorrow which taints past joys, making remorse wait upon the memory of bliss, and linking love and fancied guilt in such fearful society as that of the tyrant when he bound a living body to a corpse. Suddenly a thought darted into her mind. At first she rejected it as puerile and superstitious; but it would not be driven away. She called hastily for her attendant. "Manon," she said, "didst thou ever sleep on St. Catherine's couch?"

Manon crossed herself. "Heaven forefend! None ever did, since I was born, but two: one fell into the Loire and was drowned; the other only looked upon the narrow bed, and returned to her own home without a word. It is an awful place; and if the votary have not led a pious and good life, woe betide the hour when she rests her head on the holy stone!"

Constance crossed herself also. "As for our lives, it is only through our Lord and the blessed saints that we can any of us hope for righteousness. I will sleep on that couch to-morrow night!"

"Dear, my lady! and the king arrives to-morrow."

"The more need that I resolve. It cannot be that misery so intense should dwell in any heart, and no cure be found. I had hoped to be the bringer of peace to our houses; and is the good work to be for me a crown of thorns? Heaven shall direct me. I will rest to-morrow night on St. Catherine's bed: and if, as I have heard, the saint deigns to direct her votaries in dreams, I will be guided by her; and, believing that I act according to the dictates of Heaven, I shall feel resigned even to the worst."

The king was on his way to Nantes from Paris, and he slept on this night at a castle but a few miles distant. Before dawn a young cavalier was introduced into his chamber. The knight had a serious, nay, a sad aspect; and all beautiful as he was in feature and limb, looked wayworn and haggard. He stood silent in Henry's presence, who, alert and gay, turned his lively blue eyes upon his guest, saying gently, "So thou foundest her obdurate, Gaspar?"

"I found her resolved on our mutual misery. Alas! my liege, it is not, credit me, the least of my grief, that Constance sacrifices her own happiness when she destroys mine."

"And thou believest that she will say nay to the gaillard chevalier whom we ourselves present to her?"

"Oh, my liege, think not that thought! it cannot be. My heart deeply, most deeply, thanks you for your generous condescension. But she whom her lover's voice in solitude – whose entreaties, when memory and seclusion aided the spell – could not persuade, will resist even your majesty's commands. She is bent upon entering a cloister; and I, so please you, will now take my leave: – I am henceforth a soldier of the cross."

"Gaspar," said the monarch, "I know woman better than thou. It is not by submission nor tearful plaints she is to be won. The death of her relatives naturally sits heavy at the young countess's heart; and nourishing in solitude her regret and her repentance, she fancies that Heaven itself forbids your union. Let the voice of the world reach her – the voice of earthly power and earthly kindness – the one commanding, the other pleading, and both finding response in her own heart – and by my fay and the Holy Cross, she will be yours. Let our plan still hold. And now to horse: the morning wears, and the sun is risen."

The king arrived at the bishop's palace, and proceeded forthwith to mass in the cathedral. A sumptuous dinner succeeded, and it was afternoon before the monarch proceeded through the town beside the Loire to where, a little above Nantes, the Chateau Villeneuve was situated. The young countess received him at the gate. Henry looked in vain for the cheek blanched by misery, the aspect of downcast despair which he had been taught to expect. Her cheek was flushed, her manner animated, her voice scarce tremulous. "She loves him not," thought Henry, "or already her heart has consented."

A collation was prepared for the monarch; and after some little hesitation, arising even from the cheerfulness of her mien, he mentioned the name of Gaspar. Constance blushed instead of turning pale, and replied very quickly, "To-morrow, good my liege; I ask for a respite but until to-morrow; – all will then be decided; – to-morrow I am vowed to God – or"—

She looked confused, and the king, at once surprised and pleased, said, "Then you hate not young De Vaudemont; – you forgive him for the inimical blood that warms his veins."

"We are taught that we should forgive, that we should love our enemies," the countess replied, with some trepidation.

"Now, by Saint Denis, that is a right welcome answer for the novice," said the king, laughing. "What ho! my faithful serving-man, Dan Apollo in disguise! come forward, and thank your lady for her love."

In such disguise as had concealed him from all, the cavalier had hung behind, and viewed with infinite surprise the demeanour and calm countenance of the lady. He could not hear her words: but was this even she whom he had seen trembling and weeping the evening before? – this she whose very heart was torn by conflicting passion? – who saw the pale ghosts of parent and kinsman stand between her and the lover whom more than her life she adored? It was a riddle hard to solve. The king's call was in unison with his impatience, and he sprang forward. He was at her feet; while she, still passion-driven, overwrought by the very calmness she had assumed, uttered one cry as she recognised him, and sank senseless on the floor.

All this was very unintelligible. Even when her attendants had brought her to life, another fit succeeded, and then passionate floods of tears; while the monarch, waiting in the hall, eyeing the half-eaten collation, and humming some romance in commemoration of woman's waywardness, knew not how to reply to Vaudemont's look of bitter disappointment and anxiety. At length the countess' chief attendant came with an apology: "Her lady was ill, very ill The next day she would throw herself at the king's feet, at once to solicit his excuse, and to disclose her purpose."

"To-morrow – again to-morrow! – Does to-morrow bear some charm, maiden?" said the king. "Can you read us the riddle, pretty one? What strange tale belongs to to-morrow, that all rests on its advent?"

Manon coloured, looked down, and hesitated. But Henry was no tyro in the art of enticing ladies' attendants to disclose their ladies' counsel. Manon was besides frightened by the countess' scheme, on which she was still obstinately bent, so she was the more readily induced to betray it. To sleep in St. Catherine's bed, to rest on a narrow ledge overhanging the deep rapid Loire, and if, as was most probable, the luckless dreamer escaped from falling into it, to take the disturbed visions that such uneasy slumber might produce for the dictate of Heaven, was a madness of which even Henry himself could scarcely deem any woman capable. But could Constance, her whose beauty was so highly intellectual, and whom he had heard perpetually praised for her strength of mind and talents, could she be so strangely infatuated! And can passion play such freaks with us? – like death, levelling even the aristocracy of the soul, and bringing noble and peasant, the wise and foolish, under one thraldom? It was strange – yet she must have her way. That she hesitated in her decision was much; and it was to be hoped that St. Catherine would play no ill-natured part. Should it be otherwise, a purpose to be swayed by a dream might be influenced by other waking thoughts. To the more material kind of danger some safeguard should be brought.

There is no feeling more awful than that which invades a weak human heart bent upon gratifying its ungovernable impulses in contradiction to the dictates of conscience. Forbidden pleasures are said to be the most agreeable; – it may be so to rude natures, to those who love to struggle, combat, and contend; who find happiness in a fray, and joy in the conflict of passion. But softer and sweeter was the gentle spirit of Constance; and love and duty contending crushed and tortured her poor heart. To commit her conduct to the inspirations of religion, or, if it was so to be named, of superstition, was a blessed relief. The very perils that threatened her undertaking gave a zest to it; – to dare for his sake was happiness; – the very difficulty of the way that led to the completion of her wishes at once gratified her love and distracted her thoughts from her despair. Or if it was decreed that she must sacrifice all, the risk of danger and of death were of trifling import in comparison with the anguish which would then be her portion for ever.

The night threatened to be stormy, the raging wind shook the casements, and the trees waved their huge shadowy arms, as giants might in fantastic dance and mortal broil. Constance and Manon, unattended, quitted the chateau by a postern, and began to descend the hill-side. The moon had not yet risen; and though the way was familiar to both, Manon tottered and trembled; while the countess, drawing her silken cloak round her, walked with a firm step down the steep. They came to the river's side, where a small boat was moored, and one man was in waiting. Constance stepped lightly in, and then aided her fearful companion. In a few moments they were in the middle of the stream. The warm, tempestuous, animating, equinoctial wind swept over them. For the first time since her mourning, a thrill of pleasure swelled the bosom of Constance. She hailed the emotion with double joy. It cannot be, she thought, that Heaven will forbid me to love one so brave, so generous, and so good as the noble Gaspar. Another I can never love; I shall die if divided from him; and this heart, these limbs, so alive with glowing sensation, are they already predestined to an early grave? Oh no! life speaks aloud within them. I shall live to love. Do not all things love? – the winds as they whisper to the rushing waters? the waters as they kiss the flowery banks, and speed to mingle with the sea? Heaven and earth are sustained by, and live through, love; and shall Constance alone, whose heart has ever been a deep, gushing, overflowing well of true affection, be compelled to set a stone upon the fount to lock it up for ever?

These thoughts bade fair for pleasant dreams; and perhaps the countess, an adept in the blind god's lore, therefore indulged them the more readily. But as thus she was engrossed by soft emotions, Manon caught her arm: – "Lady, look," she cried; "it comes – yet the oars have no sound. Now the Virgin shield us! Would we were at home!"

A dark boat glided by them. Four rowers, habited in black cloaks, pulled at oars which, as Manon said, gave no sound; another sat at the helm: like the rest, his person was veiled in a dark mantle, but he wore no cap; and though his face was turned from them, Constance recognised her lover. "Gaspar," she cried aloud, "dost thou live?" – but the figure in the boat neither turned its head nor replied, and quickly it was lost in the shadowy waters.

How changed now was the fair countess' reverie! Already Heaven had begun its spell, and unearthly forms were around, as she strained her eyes through the gloom. Now she saw and now she lost view of the bark that occasioned her terror; and now it seemed that another was there, which held the spirits of the dead; and her father waved to her from shore, and her brothers frowned on her.

Meanwhile they neared the landing. Her bark was moored in a little cove, and Constance stood upon the bank. Now she trembled, and half yielded to Manon's entreaty to return; till the unwise suivante mentioned the king's and De Vaudemont's name, and spoke of the answer to be given to-morrow. What answer, if she turned back from her intent?

She now hurried forward up the broken ground of the bank, and then along its edge, till they came to a hill which abruptly hung over the tide. A small chapel stood near. With trembling fingers the countess drew forth the key and unlocked its door. They entered. It was dark – save that a little lamp, flickering in the wind, showed an uncertain light from before the figure of

Saint Catherine. The two women knelt; they prayed; and then rising, with a cheerful accent the countess bade her attendant good-night. She unlocked a little low iron door. It opened on a narrow cavern. The roar of waters was heard beyond. "Thou mayest not follow, my poor Manon," said Constance, – "nor dost thou much desire: – this adventure is for me alone."

It was hardly fair to leave the trembling servant in the chapel alone, who had neither hope nor fear, nor love, nor grief to beguile her; but, in those days, esquires and waiting-women often played the part of subalterns in the army, gaining knocks and no fame. Besides, Manon was safe in holy ground. The countess meanwhile pursued her way groping in the dark through the narrow tortuous passage. At length what seemed light to her long-darkened sense gleamed on her. She reached an open cavern in the overhanging hill's side, looking over the rushing tide beneath. She looked out upon the night. The waters of the Loire were speeding, as since that day have they ever sped – changeful, yet the same; the heavens were thickly veiled with clouds, and the wind in the trees was as mournful and ill-omened as if it rushed round a murderer's tomb. Constance shuddered a little, and looked upon her bed, – a narrow ledge of earth and a moss-grown stone bordering on the very verge of the precipice. She doffed her mantle, – such was one of the conditions of the spell; – she bowed her head, and loosened the tresses of her dark hair; she bared her feet; and thus, fully prepared for suffering to the utmost the chill influence of the cold night, she stretched herself on the narrow couch that scarce afforded room for her repose, and whence, if she moved in sleep, she must be precipitated into the cold waters below.

At first it seemed to her as if she never should sleep again. No great wonder that exposure to the blast and her perilous position should forbid her eyelids to close. At length she fell into a reverie so soft and soothing that she wished even to watch; and then by degrees her senses became confused; and now she was on St. Catherine's bed – the Loire rushing beneath, and the wild wind sweeping by – and now – oh whither? – and what dreams did the saint send, to drive her to despair, or to bid her be blest for ever?

Beneath the rugged hill, upon the dark tide, another watched, who feared a thousand things, and scarce dared hope. He had meant to precede the lady on her way, but when he found that he had outstayed his time, with muffled oars and breathless haste he had shot by the bark that contained his Constance, nor even turned at her voice, fearful to incur her blame, and her commands to return. He had seen her emerge from the passage, and shuddered as she leant over the cliff. He saw her step forth, clad as she was in white, and could mark her as she lay on the ledge beetling above. What a vigil did the lovers keep! – she given up to visionary thoughts, he knowing – and the consciousness thrilled his bosom with strange emotion – that love, and love for him, had led her to that perilous couch; and that while dangers surrounded her in every shape, she was alive only to the small still voice that whispered to her heart the dream which was to decide their destinies. She slept perhaps – but he waked and watched, and night wore away, as, now praying, now entranced by alternating hope and fear, he sat in his boat, his eyes fixed on the white garb of the slumberer above.

Morning – was it morning that struggled in the clouds? Would morning ever come to waken her? And had she slept? and what dreams of weal or woe had peopled her sleep? Gaspar grew impatient. He commanded his boatmen still to wait, and he sprang forward, intent on clambering the precipice. In vain they urged the danger, nay, the impossibility of the attempt; he clung to the rugged face of the hill, and found footing where it would seem no footing was. The acclivity, indeed, was not high; the dangers of St. Catherine's bed arising from the likelihood that any one who slept on so narrow a couch would be precipitated into the waters beneath. Up the steep ascent Gaspar continued to toil, and at last reached the roots of a tree that grew near the summit. Aided by its branches, he made good his stand at the very extremity of the ledge, near the pillow on which lay the uncovered head of his beloved. Her hands were folded on her bosom; her dark hair fell round her throat and pillowed her cheek; her face was serene: sleep was there in all its innocence and in all its helplessness; every wilder emotion was hushed, and her bosom heaved in regular breathing. He could see her heart beat as it lifted her fair hands crossed above. No statue hewn of marble in monumental effigy was ever half so fair; and within that surpassing form dwelt a soul true, tender, self-devoted, and affectionate as ever warmed a human breast.

With what deep passion did Gaspar gaze, gathering hope from the placidity of her angel countenance! A smile wreathed her lips; and he too involuntarily smiled, as he hailed the happy omen; when suddenly her cheek was flushed, her bosom heaved, a tear stole from her dark lashes, and then a whole shower fell, as starting up she cried, "No! – he shall not die! – I will unloose his chains! – I will save him!" Gaspar's hand was there. He caught her light form ready to fall from the perilous couch. She opened her eyes and beheld her lover, who had watched over her dream of fate, and who had saved her.

Manon also had slept well, dreaming or not, and was startled in the morning to find that she waked surrounded by a crowd. The little desolate chapel was hung with tapestry – the altar adorned with golden chalices – the priest was chanting mass to a goodly array of kneeling knights. Manon saw that King Henry was there; and she looked for another whom she found not, when the iron door of the cavern passage opened, and Gaspar de Vaudemont entered from it, leading the fair form of Constance; who, in her white robes and dark dishevelled hair, with a face in which smiles and blushes contended with deeper emotion, approached the altar, and, kneeling with her lover, pronounced the vows that united them for ever.

It was long before the happy Gaspar could win from his lady the secret of her dream. In spite of the happiness she now enjoyed, she had suffered too much not to look back even with terror to those days when she thought love a crime, and every event connected with them wore an awful aspect. "Many a vision," she said, "she had that fearful night. She had seen the spirits of her father and brothers in Paradise; she had beheld Gaspar victoriously combating among the infidels; she had beheld him in King Henry's court, favoured and beloved; and she herself – now pining in a cloister, now a bride, now grateful to Heaven for the full measure of bliss presented to her, now weeping away her sad days – till suddenly she thought herself in Paynim land; and the saint herself, St Catherine, guiding her unseen through the city of the infidels. She entered a palace, and beheld the miscreants rejoicing in victory; and then, descending to the dungeons beneath, they groped their way through damp vaults, and low, mildewed passages, to one cell, darker and more frightful than the rest. On the floor lay one with soiled and tattered garments, with unkempt locks and wild, matted beard. His cheek was worn and thin; his eyes had lost their fire; his form was a mere skeleton; the chains hung loosely on the fleshless bones."

"And was it my appearance in that attractive state and winning costume that softened the hard heart of Constance!" asked Gaspar, smiling at this painting of what would never be.

"Even so," replied Constance; "for my heart whispered me that this was my doing; and who could recall the life that waned in your pulses – who restore, save the destroyer! My heart never warmed to my living, happy knight as then it did to his wasted image as it lay, in the visions of night, at my feet. A veil fell from my eyes; a darkness was dispelled from before me. Methought I then knew for the first time what life and what death was. I was bid believe that to make the living happy was not to injure the dead; and I felt how wicked and how vain was that false philosophy which placed virtue and good in hatred and unkindness. You should not die; I would loosen your chains and save you, and bid you live for love. I sprung forward, and the death I deprecated for you would, in my presumption, have been mine, – then, when first I felt the real value of life, – but that your arm was there to save me, your dear voice to bid me be blest for evermore."

www.ingramcontent.com/pod-product-compliance
Lightning Source LLC
Chambersburg PA
CBHW031240260626
47169CB00007B/2381